Acclaim for Jane Shapiro's

THE DANGEROUS HUSBAND

"Dazzling. . . . I burst out loud laughing on page 54 and couldn't stop until the end of this novel. . . . *The Dangerous Husband* provides us with a close, hard-hearted, sadly funny rereading of that old fairy tale *Beauty and the Beast*. . . . There's an enduring myth that men, in our society, can be redeemed by the love of a good woman. That myth contains two very strange beliefs: that men need, at some level, to be redeemed, and that women are good. This absolutely brilliant novel tells the story of an unredeemable man, and a wife who—almost by definition—is just as dangerous as he is."　　　　　—Carolyn See, *Washington Post Book World*

"With this simultaneously Chaplinesque and Hitchcockian little fairy tale, Jane Shapiro demonstrates once more that no one is funnier than she. This she owes to a prose style that is brilliant and succinct as a martini. She is also fluent in irony at levels that would cause most other writers to pass out."　　—Lorrie Moore

"Deeply, darkly funny."　　　　　—Liza Featherstone, *Newsday*

"Wicked. That's the only description for Jane Shapiro's novel *The Dangerous Husband,* a black comedy that will speak to anyone who has ever dwelled, briefly or at length, on how useful the death of a spouse might be. With a biting wit and a dark understanding of human motives, Shapiro strips bare the veneer of modern love and marriage to reveal an impulse to murder."　　　　　—Deirdre Donahue, *USA Today*

"A small masterpiece.... For all its zaniness, the novel is neither silly nor slight; Shapiro uses this satirical Everyday couple to contemplate the alternately comforting and destructive nature of marriage." —*Mademoiselle*

"*The Dangerous Husband* is a hilarious venture into urban connubial 'noir.'" —*Des Moines Register*

"Jane Shapiro's *The Dangerous Husband* is a wicked, devastatingly funny comedy of manners. It will be perceived very differently by women and men, and who can say which sex will decode it more accurately?" —Joyce Carol Oates

"Shapiro's sense of tension-packed dialogue and staccato timing can endow a periodontal appointment or an encounter with a Guardian Angel impersonator with the sharpest pinpoints of drama, and she gets understatement, nuance, and squirming irony as well as anyone writing at the moment.... Shapiro will get you right where it hurts."

—Margaria Fichtner, *Miami Herald*

"There has been a great industry dedicated to the literature of disaster and survival. But tales of drowned sailors and snowbound stragglers pale before *The Dangerous Husband,* a wildly intelligent, funny, charming, and unsettling—or unsettlingly charming—work of psychosexual suspense. What could be more horrifying than sleeping with a man who tracks mud into the house? Jane Shapiro is a magnificent comic and an elegant, natural stylist, and reading her is pure joy." —Donald Antrim

"Shapiro's observations about relationships are priceless."

—Jill Smolowe, *People*

"Her narrator is manic, and her prose is also lusty. *The Dangerous Husband* is a very wet book. There's lots of sex, both real and imagined, as well as profuse sweating and humidity that's so present and various, it's almost a main character."

—Kristin Van Ogtrop, *Vogue*

"A beautifully written tale of whirlwind courtship and doomed love.... Shapiro has prodigious talent."

—Susan Dunne, *Hartford Courant*

"Is Jane Shapiro Laurie Colwin's evil twin, or did she somehow manage to channel Jane Austen and Edgar Allen Poe simultaneously? Either way, *The Dangerous Husband* is a singular achievement, the first of a whole new genre—postfeminist slapstick tragicomedy—as entertaining as it is disturbing."

—Kurt Andersen

"Truth may be stranger than fiction but never this clever—a lethal little novel disguised as nothing but the truth . . . watch yourself: The ending's got bite."   —Carolyn White, *Mirabella*

THE
DANGEROUS
HUSBAND

THE
DANGEROUS
HUSBAND

a novel

JANE SHAPIRO

Little, Brown and Company

BOSTON   NEW YORK   LONDON

Originally published in hardcover by
Little, Brown and Company, September 1999

First Back Bay paperback edition, September 2000

The characters and events in this book are fictitious. Any similarity to real persons,
living or dead, is coincidental and not intended by the author.

It is a pleasure to thank the Corporation of Yaddo
and the New Jersey State Council on the Arts for their support.

Library of Congress Cataloging-in-Publication Data
Shapiro, Jane.
        The dangerous husband : a novel / Jane Shapiro.
— 1st ed.
            p.   cm.
        ISBN 0-316-78247-5 (hc) / 0-316-78265-3 (pb)
        I. Title.
    PS3560.H34118D36   1999
    813'.54 — dc21   99-21424

10 9 8 7 6 5 4 3 2 1

Q-FF

Book design by Melodie Wertelet

Printed in the United States of America

For Julia Henckel Shapiro

PART I

1

We were introduced at one of those theatrical, poignant Manhattan Thanksgivings, a splendid party (singular guests, including small precocious chess-playing children and a cousin of Jim Jarmusch's; cornucopia of gourds and wildflowers pouring down the center of the trestle table; old family silver bought at a yard sale in Maine) in the clever, threadbare Horatio Street home of our shared acquaintance Lydia, a magazine editor who bravely orchestrates holiday feasts for the friends who have become her family and always takes in strays: This guy and I were the strays.

"Help me," he said in greeting. "I'm in a mess."

"I'm not the one to save you!" I snapped, and we laughed like maniacs.

He was holding his canapé plate as though clutching a railing and tipping white wine onto his trousers; my first act as his new friend was to swab with my cocktail napkin at his attractive lap. I had just finished recuperating from a romance with a fellow photographer that had ended as badly as expected — a bolter, and he bolted. Then, in a convalescent mood, I'd been taking some walks alongside a large psychiatric social worker and seeing some French movies with a small, wiry urologist, and these goalless activities had grown too noticeably noncommital for everybody involved; we were all three of us, medium, short, and tall, depressed, you may think, and maybe so. I had figured this was maturity — the end of gullibility, exaggerated expectations, being in a rush. Still, I occasionally caught myself in a sort of prayer: Somebody come to me. All these years and I had never managed to be married. This guy with the spilled wine, for his part, as I would learn immediately, was imagining his own new life, nothing involving any woman — he was going to write a novel.

"I'm so bad at impression management," he said.

" 'Impression management'? Are you making a joke?"

"I'm thinking about Erving Goffman — sociologist who wrote *Asylums*? Goffman also wrote more interestingly than anybody about almost everything that happens when people get together, including spilling your drink. He's dead now. It's a real loss."

"I'm sorry." Suddenly I was aware of being stupidly charmed, as in the presence of, say, Sting, or Danny DeVito.

"Even though I only met him once, Goffman was my mentor."

"Okay, tell me."

Our first topic, then, Erving Goffman, late hero. Goffman who brilliantly delineates the ways in which social situations offer opportunities to convey flattering information about oneself even as those same occasions are inevitably risky times when unflattering information may be revealed — say, perhaps, about one's physical aplomb or lack thereof, he told me, grinning, standing slightly bent with the big wet spot on the front of his slacks. "Goffman himself was incapable of attending a dinner party without making the hostess cry." Goffman who in his book *Interaction Ritual* quotes an assertion attributed to Karl Wallenda on the subject of returning to the high wire after the Wallenda troupe's fatal accident in Detroit: "To be on the wire is life. The rest is waiting." I was excited. Yes, the time is now — I will inch out on the wire! I gazed into the man's beautiful, fast-darkening eyes. Is this guy getting an erection? I asked myself, with the normal admixture of fear and hope, as together we prepared to kiss the past good-bye.

"Take a walk with me," he said, "and we'll start our conversation."

Once around the block at a measured pace through gray November air, doing some of the talking we'd apparently been saving up all our years for just such a moment.

How long ago it seems. We were chatting our little hearts out.

I told him about my first photograph, shot in 1971 in subway light at the Thirty-fourth Street station with my first range finder, when I was nineteen: an old man and an old woman sharing a laugh.

I told him about my thumbprint cyanotypes — to this day, I still love the giant whorls swirling lusciously in all that beautiful nineteenth-century blueness. "Hands have been used by artists in so many cultures," I averred, straining to attach some perhaps tenuous but nonetheless arguably genuine sociological (or possibly anthropological — still in the ballpark) import to my work. As we rounded the first corner, he held my wrist, causing me to blurt out useless technical information: "The paper is prepared with ferric ammonium citrate and potassium ferrous cyanide, dried away from bright light!" I wanted to forestall his thinking, For the last five years this woman has been taking pictures of her thumb. And, strolling at his side through an arcadian Greenwich Village, I saw myself breaking free of hitherto unfelt chains: *I've worked with blue too long.*

As soon as we met, in short, we fell in love. It hit us hard, the way love is supposed to, here in America. It made us feel nauseated and carry ourselves tenderly. Sudden passion. Unlooked-for communion. Hope of repair.

When sociologist Erving Goffman speaks of *fatefulness,* this is surely what he means. Secretly we were starved twins, suddenly at the end of our lifelong search for our other halves. We were forty years old and, now I see, immaculate.

*

Back at Lydia's, we switched the placecards in order to sit side by side. He shoved my chair under me with a refreshing disregard for ceremony, and we talked on.

"Goffman was really a symbolic interactionist," he murmured, "and a dramaturge. He understood that our interactions with each other are symbolic, and that their purposes are twofold: one, to further our aims. And, two, and crucially, to save face."

"Go on."

"Here's the great thing Goffman revealed: Life is lived in the evocative tense."

"What does that mean?"

"That the self is situationally constructed. That, by and large, people are not, as they imagine themselves to be, governed by an inner core of values."

"That's only half right," I whispered. "Do you believe that literally? You wouldn't deny that *some* of our values *are* absolute and *do* determine how we act. There are certain things you and I know we simply would not do."

"Yes," he whispered, "you think that, of course. Goffman illustrates how you're wrong. Goffman shows the ways in which our rational ideas about our values and goals are always secondary to ego protection. What makes him fascinating is his depiction of a huge variety of face-saving mechanisms."

"No no," I whispered. "In social situations, yes. But in more serious matters, ultimately our values *are* going to determine what we do. They just are."

"You'd be surprised," he whispered.

"Well, no I would not," I whispered, with that urgent womanly sincerity that bespeaks sexual arousal.

He countered with a frankly masculine grin, appreciative, indulgent, and calm.

My underpants seemed dampish. Actually, why were we whispering? This was a dinner table and we were entitled to have dinner conversation! "Look," I whispered. "Here's something I know: I am not going to kill. I mean unless it was in some extreme self-defense situation, to save my own life, and that's just normal. Otherwise, even if I felt abused or victimized, believe me, I'm not murdering anybody."

"Sure you are, if your ego is sufficiently threatened. You'll suddenly find that you —"

"Are you actually maintaining, in a more than theoretical way, that people, in real life, if their 'ego is threatened,' will —"

"What I'm saying," he whispered, "and all I'm saying, is that people are more collaborators with each other than they are individuals guided by a moral compass. What Goffman demonstrates are the myriad ways this gets played out — the number of gestures we make, the repertoire of gestures —"

Somewhere there was a musical clinking and a thick silence fell. I whispered, "I understand you're *trying* to say that we —"

"*Hel-lo?*" a woman — our hostess! — sang.

As one, we looked up. All down the table, faces were smiling at us in the candlelight, the fresh pink faces of twenty unfamiliar, apparently friendly but completely uninformed persons, waiting in vain for my beloved and me to find our way back to their pale and irrelevant world. After a long moment spent gazing at us, they applauded.

Of course we ate almost nothing, he and I. When the pumpkin pie and apple crisp were passed, we were still animated, still fresh. Candles low and guttering. The other guests, strangers all, lolling around us obtunded with tryptophan. We talked on.

I tasted a tiny drip of whipped cream with my finger. He shifted his foot and I glanced under the table. Brand-new highly polished palomino-colored wingtip. He rested its edge against the edge of my boot, and I can tell you I felt his heart beating like mine, through two layers of shoe leather and hose.

2

The week I first encountered him was the week he got fired. He didn't mention what his superiors at the university said when they precipitously let him go, but obviously it was unjust: Clearly he was a lovely guy, brave and warm. They locked him out of the building! (This after a thankless decade of reverse commuting. That's a New Jersey college for you — they're nuts over there.) That was only two years ago now, long and contorted years as it would turn out — before I knew him, before I married him, before I planned his death. My future husband, for that's what he was, decided the hell with sociology, there was an embryo inside him squeaking to emerge, he would finally stay home and just get this novel birthed.

He had inherited money. This news, I admit, enhanced my attraction to him, which as you know was already spirited and heartfelt. (Frankly, I'll also admit parenthetically, our meeting couldn't have happened at a more helpful moment. I'd been struggling to pay my rent all those years in New York, shooting for magazines and occasionally for somebody's book jacket, and I was tired and I was broke. Now perhaps I would be rich.) His paternal grandfather had arrived on Ellis Island at sixteen, forgotten Russian, abandoned Yiddish, made several million 1930s dollars in commercial real estate, outlived his wife and son, written a succinct will lavishly gifting his only grandchild, and died an old man, extremely rich and dark of mood, far from home. Thus begins our life together: Without his grandfather, we couldn't have afforded it.

My lover lived surprisingly modestly for such a wealthy man, but still he lived well, and, in the way the rich do, he slept without fear. And in the midst of the recent bruising episode at the college — obviously, I thought, one of those innocent miscommunications that had escalated into a brouhaha which, while this sweet guy must've watched stunned and powerless, had transmogrified into a brutal, backstabbing, academic-jungle debacle — at the point he realized *I have to get out of this situation,* he, unlike most people, could afford to do just that. He could spend a modest fraction of his wealth to change himself from a sociologist ("Whatever that is," he said grimly) into a novelist ("Whatever *that* is," he chuckled). When I met him, as I say, he had begun.

What a relief for the guy to be out of that collegiate hellhole in the cramped and bitter state of New Jersey and ensconced in his study at the top of his Brooklyn brownstone. The study's four walls were hung with sheets of manila paper with Post-it notes clinging to them, these papers large and small outlining, in felt-tipped-pen iridescence in his surprisingly flamboyant script, the trajectory of the plot, the complex personality traits and ambivalences and intensely felt desires of the central characters, the physical appearances and verbal tics of the secondary characters, the chapter breakdown, and alternative ideas for the dedication, which however finally phrased would in any case lovingly commemorate Erving Goffman, most especially to honor that classic *The Presentation of Self in Everyday Life,* with its seminal section on the topic, dear, apparently, to my future husband's heart and central to his novel, of what Goffman calls "performance disruption — unmeant gestures, inopportune intrusions, faux pas, and scenes." Such a great room. From this busy third-floor atelier you would've seen the East River and Manhattan beyond, had the windows not been entirely concealed behind additional charts describing the novel's key moments and their respective chronologies and microchronologies to the extent the novelist had conceived them so far. As I feel I want to say again, the windows were covered: Without a moment's hesitation, my new lover had converted a treetop room with a priceless view into a camera obscura, a dark and bristling cave.

This was adorable. The rug teemed with crumpled scraps bearing inferior and rejected paragraphs. On our first date, the day after Lydia's Thanksgiving, my new lover and I waded into the scraps and stood there ankle deep, gazing around in the lively gloom, and imagined some future together, stretching before us like an expanse of calm and deepening water.

The second week in December found us in Jamaica, sportif in white linen (twin outfits) and dancing on a terrace strung with Christmas lights under a Caribbean moon. Scent of choice marijuana, the cream of the winter crop. Warm wind. The sea blackly glittering.

He was a happy dancer, groundlessly confident, with only an intermittent interest in the rhythms being maintained by four impassive, stoned, gifted musicians who shared an attitude that was part nurturance, part challenge: If you dance forever, we play forever. He executed fancy steps according to a cadence known only to him. I happen to follow well. I'll never leave him, I suddenly thought. He whirled us and I clung like lichen.

As the night wore on and we two continued to hold the floor, the combo abandoned ballads for reggae, but we were too crafty for these transparent individuals, who obviously hoped to destabilize us by the shift of musical genre. We continued to dance entwined as though they were still playing jazz standards in the cruise-ship vernacular — *Poinciana, your branches speak to me of love.* The moon set, and he and I were alone under the black and starry sky. As I'm aware is not uncommon among people enjoying expensive Caribbean vacations, I felt I had come home.

*

Yes, we first came together during the magical, violent, and demoralizing holiday season, creatively transforming it into a time of joy and rebirth.

Hanukkah arrived, and in an access of expansiveness we agreed to go ahead and celebrate. The first night, I stood in a sort of whole-body distension, in a vaporous weakness, lighting the single candle and thinking about his incomparable touch, so strong, so hot. In the menorah's flickering light, faintly brighter every evening, at my instigation we held hands, safe at last. I unwrapped tiny expensive gifts, he unwrapped tiny cheap ones.

Christmas came, and we joined the volunteers outside Grand Central Station distributing peanut-butter sandwiches, cartons of milk, and sticks of cheese to four hundred polite people without resources. (United in guilt, concern, and a new sense of possibility, we determined to do much more in the months ahead.) After that we weren't ready to go indoors, because we could. Midnight found us back in Brooklyn and strolling through Carroll Gardens in its seasonal artificial daylight — tremendous wattage in the yards, thousands of bulbs pouring light all over the crèches and Rudolphs and the entire secure family neighborhood, and me and my lover already a family of two.

As the new year approached, we planned a party.

Last night of the year, first of our life — that's what we knew. Music and fireplace blazing and canapés on wafer-like trays being rushed here and there by teenagers in butchers' aprons portraying waiters. My lover popped the corks on thirty bottles of Veuve Cliquot and lined up the bottles on the high front stoop in the snow. The brownstone's door stood open, and our friends kept climbing the steps and bursting in with cold air transpiring from their coats, stepping from icy darkness into the bright and enveloping warmth of the life my lover and I had suddenly, almost immediately upon laying eyes on each other, begun to create.

I looked great. I loved my expensive new velvet dress and kept sneaking a feel of it. My hairdo was shiny and wild, black snake tendrils shot with silvery gray. Standing in the foyer greeting people, I was seeing what awaited us: our babies tousled and sweet-eyed; our children in their Hopalong Cassidy pajamas singing along with Mouseketeers on a Philco TV (in a mild champagne confusion, I had accidentally been transported back to the 1950s, his and mine); our shared geriatric years as a sexually engaged and wise couple in some lovely city not unlike Paris. When we were old I would still be a photographer but a mature artist come into her own; he would still be a novelist and, though literally shorter than now, a man of towering moral stature. Gone, as I stood there, were my nerve-racking only-child childhood, my cramped Bank Street apartment, my numerous fruitless dates with other hopeful beings. I fingered the velvet dress: I am here.

Two hours in the front hall, overexcited, cold and hot. My lover's squash partner, Pudney, said in greeting, "Where's the phone?" and rushed to the kitchen on snowy sneakered feet. My lover's veterinarian, red-haired Mona, looked at me with real curiosity. Arriving next, Donald, my oldest friend, set down his congas, took me in his arms, and murmured, "I'm glad for you," which caused me, already overwrought, to begin to cry, whereupon my lover rushed up behind us shouting, *"Unhand her!"* and then shook Donald's hand and clapped him on the back for a long thumping time while we all laughed giddily.

As if with water steadily rising, the house filled. The windows steamed over. Coats piled up on the bed.

"Wait right here," my lover said.

Nearby in the crowd was my friend Sallie, who was known for aggressiveness, generosity, and always being interested. I had things to tell her, but my lover had said "Wait," and, in an unmistakably erotic way, I wanted to obey him. While I was thus stuck to the carpet, a youngish-oldish man slid up to Sallie, introduced himself, and told her a piece of his story: "Do you cook? This is where I dine, at parties or in restaurants; my own idea of making supper is to grill some toast."

"Never mind that, I need to ask you something," Sallie said in her large voice, and she grabbed him by the belt and dragged him away; then it was obvious she was talking about me and my lover.

Other people came and went. I stood still. Nobody spoke to me, the hostess, although half the guests were friends of mine. For a while I waited there, thinking about the man who grilled his toast points and hoping he would find somebody to cure his hunger, as I had. I waited a long time. My lover didn't come back.

Also at the party were my lover's putative immediate precursors in my life, those two with whom I had shared that time of unacknowledged waiting, the six-foot-six-inch social worker, unfortunately unable to be a full participant in the party on account of being so tall, and the five-foot-four-inch urologist, who arrived with a brand-new girlfriend, clearly much better suited to him than I could ever have been, a tiny woman in a tiny green silk gown. Neither of these men, towering or minuscule, appeared to begrudge me my new happiness. But if I hadn't known better, I almost would have said that they were avoiding me.

And Lydia was there, at whose Thanksgiving dinner we had met, and her former girlfriend Susan, a tennis pro with beautiful big forearms. And so many others, all of them remarkable, all of them great. The women with their long dresses and flushed faces and bright eyes. A small, cheerful, incredibly intelligent man, provost of an undistinguished college, was crouched in the kitchen sink refusing to get out. The noise rose, people mobbed the buffet, champagne splashed. I went looking for my lover and found him, and then we just stood, in the midst of everything, in each other's arms, and I laid my head on his shoulder as though resting for the first time. We loved each other and our love was bleeding all over the house. That is to say, we admired ourselves and our guests. We adored them all. They were the best the world has ever known.

Just before midnight he grabbed a champagne flute and clinked it, and yelled into the sudden silence. "I want us to raise a glass to — Lydia? Where's Lydia? I just want us to raise a glass to the woman who's actually responsible for this party happening. She made it happen by giving a Thanksgiving dinner herself, where — Lyd, don't hide, I want to talk to you. Thank you, Susan, good, push her forward. C'mon, sweetie, let me toast you. Okay, Lydia is the person who introduced me to the most remarkable woman I've ever met, and I have to say I will always be grateful to Lydia who has given me the kind of gift I wish every one of you could receive in this new year," and so on. Somewhere in the middle of this speech, Lydia suddenly sat down, fell over on the couch, and buried her head under a throw pillow. The tennis pro removed the pillow with economical athlete's gestures and gently stood her up. "It was you," my lover was saying, his champagne aloft and fizzing. "You made something happen for me which has transformed my life completely, *and I have to say I think permanently*" — murmurs from the crowd — "in the most wonderful way. You did it, Lyd."

"I did not introduce these two people," Lydia said, oddly. Technically this was correct, but why bring it up? Neither of us, truth to tell, had known Lydia long, and now she was making a bit of a spectacle of herself, trying to pull her arm out of Susan's masterful grip and saying fretfully over and over, "But I didn't introduce them."

Still, standing among our benign and eager celebrants, all of us rosy and now frankly sweating, I was as happy as I've been. This Lydia might blush in disclaimer but she had given us everything. Everybody sipped and screamed and kissed, and midnight came and the ball crashed to earth.

3

New Year's Day 1993, the first day of the first full year of our lives in each other's protection, dawned darkly with fine snow swirling. I woke already gazing at him, his curly head on the pillow, his arm thrown back. I watched in a haze of feelings wonderfully combined, that lover's mix of tenderness, gratitude, suppressed anxiety, and lust. Slept again, and woke, alone — already wondering, Where is he? — into a bright gray January first, foggy, visibility about two feet.

An hour later, Sallie called. She was my closest woman friend in the city, and when I had first arrived we had shared darkroom space and collaborated on a couple of projects. In our best series, we had persuaded one hundred men, all ages and sizes and miens, to let us do their head prints. Almost all of them were friends and acquaintances of Sallie's; twelve were mine. We got each man to lean over and press his right cheek to a sheet of sixteen-by-twenty contact photographic paper and hold still for twenty seconds while we exposed the paper, and the left side of his head, to full-spectrum light. Of course this produced silhouettes — bright cloudy white on black. Sometimes they were factual portraits: You recognized the subject's profile at once, or his inimitable hair, or some other telling aspect of his look or character. And other times, no matter how well you knew or loved the guy, you could not find him at all.

"I talked with Cooper last night," Sallie said. "We're both a little concerned about you."

"Who's Cooper?"

"Your friend Cooper. *I* don't know who he is. That nice WASPy guy, in the bow tie."

"I think I saw him talking to you. But I don't know him."

"He knows *you*," Sallie said.

"No, he doesn't."

"Well, didn't you invite him?"

"No."

"That's so strange. I thought he was expressing the same concern I'm feeling."

"I never met the guy."

Sallie said, "Well, now I don't know what to say."

"What were these concerns?"

"I'm wondering if —" She stopped.

"What?"

In an uncharacteristic halting rhythm, she tried to spit it out: that perhaps she was misguided, but an odd feeling she had was so intractable and intense, she hoped I wouldn't take offense, but she could see I was getting deeper into a relationship that — well, maybe she should first pose a question: Was I in love?

"Yup," I said, winsome and proud.

"Well, do you think it's serious?"

"Definitely. As serious as it gets."

Sallie said, "Well, I know you've been very lonely."

"I haven't felt that lonely," I told her. "I've just been alone. And now I'm not."

She said, "And when there are money problems, it's nice to meet a man with substantial assets."

"It's not that."

"No?"

I said finally, "Don't you like him?"

"Oh, no. I mean, I *like* him, I just —" But in her pause I heard the unmistakable sound of somebody hesitating on a threshold, then turning back. "Well, I just don't know him. But I know that if you want to be with him, he's got to be a wonderful wonderful wonderful man. And you're going to have a wonderful wonderful time."

Late at night sometimes, in this beginning, my new lover read to me. I would lie in bed swaddled in bedding, and he'd sit in the upholstered chair at my side. In his reading glasses and flannel nightshirt and leather slippers, he looked so comely and strong. The lamp's glow; his voice gaining authority; our happiness, in those precious moments, complete.

"Do you mind doing this?"

"Do I mind reading to you? Are you kidding? You're my sweetie! This is better than a blow job!"

So cute. Our faces alight. We grinned our easy complicity into each other's besotted eyes.

To put it another way, we were classically in love, holding the classic beliefs: Everything is possible between us, we can authentically care for each other through not just the coming days but, should we live long enough — and surely we will, so marvelously bolstered are our immune systems — through the numerous busy decades to come. We are one in true understanding. These brief days and nights of being given — at last, at last — everything we need, and some things we didn't know we needed, have left us fully stocked with reserves of loving-kindness, such that we — well, everybody can tell the story. It's in no way denigrating to admit what we all know: This time comes and then it goes.

My new lover had a frog, a svelte albino. Four inches long, *Xenopus leavis,* late of Kenya. Her name was Bianca and she lived in a bucket. She hung there in water, pinkish, lipless, to all appearances exhausted from treading

and waiting for rescue, staring out of tiny golden superi-
orly placed beads into the dark. My new lover ushered
me into the basement of his house, bustled over and
lifted the wooden lid, and said, "Hi, sweetheart. You
look great. Your color's terrific. I'm so glad you're not
dead!" Whenever he approached the bucket, he told me,
he was afraid the frog might've died. Gee, I thought, she
certainly might. Then he scattered pinches of frog food,
and Bianca made frantic rhythmic motions with her
arms — I mean her front legs, with their undeniably elegant, translucent webbed and clawed feet — to wrestle
the flecks of dried bloodworm to her simultaneously
intense and blank face: the only event in her life.

We stared until pale Bianca fell still. She hung there,
trapped, sated, inert. Bianca was cute but horrible. Like
the man I had fallen in love with: In that moment he
became, in some muted but unmistakable way, horrible
too. Weeks had flown while we dallied joyfully; now,
without warning, we were suddenly in that well-known
moment, the lovers' first recoil: He's *not* my beloved.
I've been so wrong.

"Albinism occurs often in rabbits, of course," he was
saying, "and occasionally even in lobsters."

"She's —"

"Terrific, huh?"

"— unnerving," I said.

"Why? She's great. She's a beautiful white frog."

"How can you keep her in a container in the dark?"

"She's happy — it's safe, it's quiet, there's water —
aren't you, cutie? This is what a frog wants: wetness and

safety and food. She likes it. She thrives. Inside her nice little home, she has become that contented frog you see. Look at that beautiful slippery skin."

"Her skin looks stretched."

"It's frog skin."

"She looks swollen."

"She's not."

"She looks it to me."

"Hey, she's really not."

"I think she's very swollen."

He said, "Hey, look. You can't expect an amphibian to be a person. She's a frog: Her skin fits her. It's smooth skin — she's almost impossible to pick up." He cracked himself up and laughed awhile. "I drop her all over the floor!"

He drops his pet? I hated him.

I waited while he jumped around in the dusk of the basement utility room, chuckling himself out. Then I said evenly, "So why did you congratulate her for not being dead?"

His stupid face clouded. "I just worry."

"You're keeping a reptile, or an amphibian, or whatever, in a bucket — you *should* worry."

"Hey, I love my frog. *The bucket is a fine environment.* It's cloistered but it's restful. She gets new water every day; I dechlorinate it, I keep it warm. It's not that she's really gonna die in there. It's not that."

"So it's what?"

"It's — I don't want to say."

I laughed, a sudden spurt of laughing, surprising in

its bitterness. Yes, I thought, this person is a seriously wrong person; but compose yourself, be measured, be adult; speak sensibly and extricate yourself in a sensible fashion; you found out in time; he's not the guy. I began, as if he were anybody — nobody: "Well, that little frog of yours —"

"The females are bigger than the males," he muttered.

"Whatever, but living under that lid definitely *might* be the end of her."

"Hey. She loves the bucket." A spasm: He hated me too.

"So, really, what do you think is going to hurt her?" I inquired with clever sweetness.

"Accident."

"She doesn't go anywhere," I pleasantly continued. "She eats; she doesn't encounter predators. She's not even very old, is she? What else, besides isolation or depression or loneliness or time, could wipe her out?"

I heard and did not hear the answer. He said: "Me."

Meanwhile, Bianca dived to the bottom, landed on her pebbles, and froze. And my future ex-lover, with a dark look, slapped the lid back on, stamped halfway up the shadowy stairs, and tripped and fell down.

That night, a night of freezing February rain, I made love with him anyway. Just sex.

We were expressive and noisy. Afterward, in the dark, as we neared sleep, with cars hissing by and splashing light across the ceiling, in the gentlest voice he had: "I think I'm keeping all my fears inside that bucket. With the lid on. In there with my Bianca."

I softened so radically the bed seemed to shift. I said, "This is not to be critical — I'm sure the frog is fine. But would it be okay if I took a few pictures of the frog?"

"Not if it's to make fun of her."

"Oh honey," I said, and, following Oh honey, all my recently acquired love for him flowed back in.

So even at the outset there are many new starts.

So this was a beginning after all.

4

Let's give him corporeal form, since he's not, after all, going anywhere. Tall, with a charming rollicking gait. A cordial and lively face. His shoulders and hands were big and strong, since he was; his hair was curly brown, his skin high-colored, his eyes light, eyelashes long, temperature hot. What a vivid guy in so many ways.

His name, now that I get around to it, was Dennis — an unprepossessing name, a disarming name in the real sense of that word. Together Dennis and I embarked on our new life. Now, these two years later, I don't know much but I'll tell you all I know. You convict me if you will.

You already see it unfolding as such things do. As almost always happens, I found out only later what had always been clear: what he was. What we were.

As with every love affair we've ever heard about in which the lovers are permitted to be together rather than being forcibly separated on account of being the children of rival clans, his other self was a betrayal; and I'm sure mine was to him.

Even this, of course, is not the end of the world. One's initial wish to flee turns out to be an overcorrection. It's a stage. Every day of the week, we know, couples are moving beyond this ordinary first moment of alarm and sudden antipathy, through ambivalence and its oscillations, blind discord and frank expressions of self-interest, then self-criticism and shame, renewed commitment to striving for perspective and fairness, reevaluation of fantastic hopes and the concomitant adjustment of expectations, growing mutual understanding, growing compassion and pride in its return, and, finally — more often than expected — uneasy and then more stable and then entirely dependable peace. No reason to think he and I couldn't walk that famous marital path. Together, we set out.

Friends would drop over, we'd stand before the fireplace sipping wine, he would run out for oysters and create a platter of angels on horseback. He'd drop his arm around my shoulders and his body would keep death away. Immortal moments, really, gazing bemusedly into the faces of our laughing pals, both of us still stunned at having so suddenly become the reliable couple we saw reflected in their eyes.

*

Insinuatingly, though, something was starting.

Dennis was becoming — how to explain? — disheveled. Affably, while chatting or cracking a joke, he might spill water, spit a crumb or two, trip over a sofa, fall off the curb. When he strolled, he occasionally walked into a wall. When he bent to attend to the laces of his running shoes, which he retied often because (now I noticed) they were rather unusually long, he might get dirt on his fingers, or catch his thumb in the knot, or start to tip and almost fall down. He righted himself with a flourish. "Nice save," he'd say.

How big a deal could such idiosyncracies be to a mature woman? Over the complicated years since adolescence, I had lost several promising men because of, now that you get down to it, having a short fuse. With Dennis I would be a finer human being. Thus I encouraged in myself, and began to rehearse, the attitude of the wise wife: implacable detached amusement commingled with dogged acceptance.

You learn nothing about a person until you see him at home. There were days when Dennis couldn't do much involving his head without bumping it. After his shower, I'd look at him from top to bottom, or bottom to top, and sometimes his toes were stubbed, or his knees scarred, or his lower half mottled with target-shaped squash-ball bruises. His hair — that thick, pretty, almost reddish little-boy hair — had three modes: curly and adorable; puffed up like a hat; or naturally spiked, as if he had got his paw stuck in the outlet. Still, this is what love is not: a fantasy about who the beloved could become. You cherish that person as himself. We've all lived long enough to know that much.

And I did love Dennis. Now that I'd noticed it, it was touching, his haplessness, sweet and funny. All that winter we both worked often at his house, to be near each other — me with my contact sheets spread on the dining table, he in reverie at his computer or wading through the balled-up papers while struggling to create pungent dialogue, hollering out sentence fragments alone in his room.

Soon, though, I had to request that he not eat any more desserts in my van. It was a Chrysler, faded and dinged; still, it was mine.

"If you want ice cream down your arm, great, but not inside my car, okay, honey?"

"No problem," he said.

Our first negotiation, and we were pleased.

We invited my old high school friend Donald and my photography partner Sallie to meet us at the Angelika for a movie. Dennis went to buy the coffees and came toddling back across the lobby through the crush of glum cineasts, finally arriving at our table with four cappuccinos in Styrofoam cups, which, while we watched entranced, he turned upside down onto his empty chair. He stared, mystified, at the gray brown puddle and its foam. "It's only coffee!" I declared, and I popped up and started swabbing. Donald and Sallie, who barely knew each other, exchanged a long and searching glance.

I didn't want to say to our friends, that day at the movies: Coffee is a problem. I do remember standing inside Dennis's spacious 1840s Brooklyn Heights house, in the slightly canted second-floor hall, on floral carpet, at noon on a February Saturday, looking out a small beveled window through snowy branches into Brooklyn, and I heard clinking from the kitchen, and my heart raced. That's all — a fibrillation, oddly like fear.

By this time I had moved in. Standing there, I was wearing one of four nightdresses that had accompanied me on the move from my infinitesimal, lightless, overpriced Bank Street one-bedroom; also with me at Dennis's were all my clothes and books and CDs, and of course my cameras and tripod and darkroom equipment, and my Rolodex and running shoes and cross-country skis, and my meditation cushion and journals and collection of tiny models of foods, and so on — in other words, my everything. And the recognition in that moment that I had brought all these things with me here to this safe and luxurious but suddenly arguably alien place made me almost see that I was in a serious bind; and there was something else I surely saw then but didn't actually think yet (though I would, of course, think it later, many times, exactly this way, about us together and each of us apart): alone in the world.

Really, I probably just stood in my new upstairs hall,

enjoying the fact that I was resident in a Greek revival house with an iron fence ornamented with pineapple finials and wondering why Dennis had to make so fucking much coffee. It was puzzling. Not scary yet. There were days when all he did was type, misplace his glasses, and brew the coffee in a machine that beeped to call him, which he didn't usually hear, so that the coffee would slowly burn and thicken until he smelled or remembered it and thumped down to the kitchen and stared into the pot and realized he'd have to start over. Strings of black dust on the kitchen counter, and mugs all around the house where they'd stay for days, continuing to cool. The curved glass of the coffeepot looked shell thin and brittle. I wonder, now, why it never got smashed; this is a mystery.

In the ensuing weeks I found myself often in that same hall in that same place, the spot that was becoming, without his or anybody else's knowing it, *my spot,* where I stood increasingly often, because while stepping into that one spot I could not be heard, on account of the carpeting, and while standing there I could not be seen, although I could see for blocks into his — our — neighborhood (which was modest, various, essentially peaceful, heavily treed, and watched over by a powerful block association in which WASPs and Jews and Italian Americans figured equally largely), and I could hear, ticking, something that was growing larger. But what? What could I hear? What could I hear? Only the ordinary activities of my lover in the house in which, genuinely side by side, my lover and I now lived.

*

I'm no saint. Around the house anybody might occasionally find herself tediously protesting: *I don't want to pick up after you. I'm not your slave.*

We squabbled awhile, withdrew some, returned to the fray refreshed, reversed direction and looked inward, said unkind things, said reparative things, wept a bit, reaffirmed our connection, formulated our shared view of our problems, resolved to improve, made promises, reconciled, and went to our room and fucked until we fainted. In bed, as it happened, his newly discovered awkwardness became wonderful abandon; he was a wildly vivacious lover, ardent, fearless, and sweet.

We wanted each other's babies.

We had weathered the first phase together and we loved each other like spent warriors.

We got married.

5

The wedding was held in the garden behind our house (which you reached by walking around the side from the front because the french doors were nailed shut — I asked why, but he never told), in garden terms at a peak moment, when Dennis's sky blue President Lincoln lilac blossoms were beginning to bloom, just before they would immediately brown and crumple and die.

Us.

And Dennis's mother, a short, intelligent, suntanned seventy-five-year-old, energetic and alert. She was so attentive during the ceremony that she vibrated; tall Donald, who was standing behind her, set his hands on her little shoulders and held her down. She and Dennis's deceased father had been older parents of this single amazing Dennis, who had been, like everybody's children, above average. Now she recalled his bar-mitzvah brightness, then stood on tiptoe to whisper to bending Donald that there was a sense in which she had recently begun to lose heart on the subject of her son. He had always done everything adorably, but messily, and late. "What a kid!" She looked game but surprisingly worried for one so far removed from the child-rearing years. She seized my hand, pressed it hard, and gazed up at me — as some mothers will at weddings — with tremendous gratitude.

And twenty other celebrants. The sanguine friends who, every one, would later be forced to abandon us. Of course we know this is what friends are: not heroes, not even fully prepared; just guests at a wedding, dressed for the occasion.

After black-and-whites and some Polaroids, I made a video. I have it still and will play it again if ever I can bear to. Flanked by azaleas, our nice people, a few years out of date in ear cuffs and Doc Martens and silk trousers, grin and raise their glasses. Clouds shift overhead, and shadows drop into the garden, where our guests feed each other tapas and, in intervals of slanting light, continue to wish us well. Sonny Rollins plays "I See Your Face Before Me" — heartbreaking melody. The breeze picks up. Waving a damask napkin, my new husband appears as himself, urgent and original and tall, and — today only, like a bride — radiant. Twice, my new husband trips and falls out of the frame.

Our honeymoon was a night on our own futon on its futon platform. We entered the bedroom and rushed each other. I was wearing a garter belt and stockings. He peeled the stockings off conscientiously, and he ripped them anyway. Of course I didn't yet know that every time my husband would touch my stockings, the whole time I'd be his wife, he would leave them in shreds. We woke simultaneously, at dawn, after an hour's sleep, deliciously battered, entangled, glistening, oddly rested. As rested as, together, he and I would ever be.

One of my favorite remarks is still Emerson's on daguerreotypes: "The artist stands aside, and lets you paint yourself."

That morning after the wedding I began the story of our new life, to be told in fifteen-by-fifteen color transparencies. I would take a few quick shots a day, in color to show the skin tones (mine yellower, his pinker), with the medium-format camera — shots of whoever was up, us or just me (my married self), or us and the orange cat, if she wasn't hiding (I didn't yet know she was never not hiding), in the south-facing alcove at the back of the dining room, in front of the nailed-shut french doors, in late-dawn light, every morning in the sequence of fresh mornings now stretching before us. I set up the tripod and shot Day 1: me, standing naked, rosy and satisfied, with distended lips. My pubic triangle is remarkably black, and I look as cheerful as one of Bellocq's friendly prostitutes. Dennis is absent but present: He is represented by a curved row of smudges inside my upper arm, four fingertip bruises as regular and natural looking as markings in fur.

Day 2: Den and me, naked and besotted, about to return to bed.

Day 3: Me and Den, naked. Me looking effortful, the long cable release in my left hand, his penis, mostly hard, in my right. Den extravagantly grinning.

Day 4: Den's hand clamped around my shoulder.

Day 5: Me behind Dennis, in shadow. Dennis, after his morning run, close up. Beautiful muscled shoulders, orange pink, gleaming. His face flushed and mettlesome, almost combative, staring the camera down. His throat beating.

Dennis was generous. A chronically openhanded guy in any season, he was now, in the aftermath of the marriage vows, almost beside himself with a single-minded and preoccupying spirit of giving. As in some fairy-tale ballet, the wedding gifts flowed for a month. He built me a darkroom in the basement. He bought me a Hasselblad. He went to a foreign section of Brooklyn in search of an opera-length strand of eleven-millimeter pearls, declining to bargain and thereby setting a precedent that amazed and thrilled the jewelry dealer, an elderly Syrian Jewish man who spent his summers seaside in an Italianate villa with topiary in Deal, New Jersey, and who with sincerity told Dennis that were the Syrian community less insular than it actually was, he would invite Dennis to visit often, since they would henceforth be friends for life. (Den carried the pearls home in his pocket, let them fall out and left them in a cab, realized in time, smashed the trunk of the cab with his hand to alert the driver to stop, *did* stop the guy, got the pearls back, took the driver out for lunch and cheerfully paid him eight hundred dollars for the freak dent in his trunk. Den's hand swelled up.) One day when he was momentarily without gift ideas, Dennis rushed out and picked up four umbrellas and a meat slicer.

"Open your present, sweetheart!" — daily. It was unusual. But nice.

He came home with a computer for me, and Photoshop software, and an Iris printer, apparently so that I could make images in the computer and print them myself and also, he supposed, maintain notes for photographs with technological assist, and he gifted me with a long patient sexy computer lesson. Later, while Den was clanking around in the kitchen cooking a surprise supper in virgin French copper pans, I climbed the stairs to peer into my new screen. I really liked sitting in my generous desk chair, in the shiny leather depression recently vacated by his generous butt.

I hadn't visited the frog Bianca since that first uneasy

time, but on my way to the darkroom I occasionally imagined removing her lid and taking a peek. Lately, I was almost always aware of Bianca in her bucket below, and of Dennis above in his study which looked as though it had been ransacked. In the computer's encyclopedia, I looked up frogs and toads.

The frog population is dying in the world.

In the United States annually, two million frogs give up their legs for entrées.

Frogs make many sounds. Sometimes almost a human scream.

Dennis was dependable. I already knew this — I had married it. Now it appeared he could also be oversolicitous.

I was getting ready to enjoy Dennis's and his grandfather's wonderful largesse, to stop freelancing to work on some montages, but before that I had to finish a last magazine shoot, in Miami Beach, of a marathon swimmer training for her next attempt to swim to Cuba inside a shark cage. We were a few weeks into our marriage, when the beloved still doesn't mind picking you up at the airport. But what passion: When I told him my schedule, Den sprang like a lion mother after an antelope, leaping up and slapping at his pockets for his car keys as if I were already in the act of arriving on the tarmac.

Evidently this guy, my husband, would pick up a loved one anywhere — airport, train or bus station, pier at dawn after a transatlantic crossing, unknown street corner in a far-flung neighborhood, Ohio — and this was how (I would discover) he did it: zoomed up, crashed to a halt, abandoned the car, slammed through the automatic door, seized the passenger's bag with titanic force, ran out again, found airport security hooking the car up for towing, jumped behind the wheel and refused to come out, hollered, apologized, peeled off big bills and dealt them all around, and drove away a satisfied man, his nose running.

I did go to Miami. The marathon swimmer greased up in sulky silence, adjusted her goggles, and moodily swam back and forth for hours, as easily as a leopard pacing a cage, in the calm pearly Atlantic, which if she could get State Department approval would soon carry her away. She was inspiring. I hung with my camera over the side of the boat. Later, while I was walking from the swimmer's hotel to mine in the steamy Florida night, a ninety-year-old man in the back of a parked Bentley opened his door and patted the seat beside him, and when I declined he looked at me with intense approval. I felt calm in Florida. With foreboding — but about what? — I flew north again.

In the airport, as I say, Dennis arrived like a fireman breaking in. "Hey! Honey, welcome back! Here, give me your bag! Give me it, give me it, I'll take it! Let's go!"

"Don't grab," I said in greeting.

"I'm just taking your bag for you!"

"I can carry it. I've *been* carrying it."

"But I want to —" He tugged at it, I held on, he pulled harder, I planted my feet and hung on with both hands. My Nikonos camera, so recently underwater, swung from my neck. "Honey, I'm just taking your —" "Don't, I'll carry it, I —" "I'll take it for you; give it —" *"Wait, don't, let go!"* *"Let me take —"* We were holding on, together, to a boat atoss in a treacherously roiling sea. Cold and sweating, grimly smiling, we were yanking for our lives.

But the pneumatic door sighed open and I glimpsed taxicabs, sunlight, the world outside. I let go and he fell down.

So Dennis was many things, several of them, of course, still wonderful. I still liked his charming unpredictability and he still liked my peppery, spicy temper. Oh, we complemented each other. His voice was bright and mine was low. His ears clogged easily; I could hear too well.

What a large and brave project. It's one of life's miracles, and people do it all the time. Night after night, day after day, in moments of levity, in solemn discussion and during dead air, my new husband and I were spinning like silkworms. We were overseeing our little factory, whose product would be us. Our union. Weaving the strands that would bind us finally and make of us what we intended to become: a couple.

In fact we would, time would show, become an utterly incomparable couple. Simultaneously, we'd turn out like every other couple that has ever existed — our strengths having become our weaknesses, our charms our flaws.

Our first wedded month was, then, as first times are, full of signs and portents.

One windy night before a storm, during a jolly quarrel, Dennis grasped my waist and sort of hefted me in his hands. I kept laughing and arguing and taking pictures, and he kept jiggling me, dropping me, hoisting me up.

Then Dennis threw me across the room. I flew over the back of a wing chair, which was upholstered in green-and-ivory-colored striped silk, and the shot I took is a blur of stripes, denim shoulder, the lamp's halation, before I held up the camera to keep it from hitting the floor. Slowly, as I flew, I thought the obvious thoughts: When I land, I could break my neck. I could be paralyzed. I could be killed.

But of course I dropped softly, safely, half on oak floor, half on the rug, as if into a carpet of lawn. Den hurled himself down beside me, whispering his entirely unnecessary apologies — I know it had been harmless horseplay! — and we lay there a long time companionably in pretty lamplight, gazing at the ceiling's plaster cornice, listening to the spring wind rushing outside our door.

Day 36: Den's leg, after running and falling. My mouth kisses his skinned knee. My hair grazes the wet new wound.

Day 37: Den happily pinching my nipple, too hard.

Day 38: Den and me, nervous.

Day 39: Den and me, pensive.

Day 40: Den and me, blurry. Behind us thick rain.

6

Dennis had a dog! Suddenly this came to light. Raleigh lived with Den's former wife, the mystery wife, about whom I had never learned anything and now will never learn anything, and two months after our wedding the mystery wife phoned (making the first of the two brief calls she would put through to our house before disappearing forever), and then Dennis murmured that the dog "might come back."

"Might come back?"

"Nothing, nothing, I spoke out of turn."

"Why so touchy?" Me, sweetly — faintly, inexplicably malicious, but sweet.

"Not touchy."

"Does this mean we might be getting this dog?"

"This means nothing. Forget about it. It could be a possibility, but I'm afraid to hope."

"Wait. I think you better tell me if you might be planning to get a dog."

"I'm not 'planning to get' anything."

"Then what are we talking about?"

"I would never get another dog," he said darkly. "I don't want any other dog."

"Do you want your former wife's dog? Is that it?"

"He's already my dog. *My* dog. Mine. Don't you want me to have him?"

"I'm asking what it is we are discussing. Who is this dog? If it's your dog, why don't you have it already?"

"He was our dog. She had custody."

"She had custody? For how long?"

"Not long."

"And now she doesn't want custody anymore?"

"Possibly not," he said unhappily. "She took my dog and now she might want to throw my dog back. My dog is the best dog in the world! How could a person give up a dog like Raleigh?"

"How did *you* give up the dog if you love it so much?"

"Quit calling him 'it'!"

I asked twenty-five questions about the animal, its size, color, temperament, provenance, history, training, relationship with Dennis, relationship with the unknown former wife, current whereabouts, eating and sleeping and outing habits, potential time of arrival in our home — all the stuff you'd ask. Slurping coffee, he gave me his full, silent attention. "This is a dog who 'might' live in our home," I said finally. Arguably somewhat canine in demeanor myself now, worrying a nice big bone. "Why the hell aren't you saying anything?"

"Why the hell are *you* calling a beloved dog 'it'?" Weird little strained smile.

I said, "You answer me. *Are* you bringing a dog in here?"

He jerked his foot as though in response to a neurologist's hammer. "Don't you think I would answer you if I could? I can't stand to! I don't want to get my hopes up! Raleigh is the nicest sweetest dog that ever existed! The day I lost Raleigh was the darkest day of my life! Raleigh is my soul mate! I love Raleigh so much! I would do anything to get Raleigh back if I could, and that's never going to happen! This is a heartbreak for me! Quit the torture!" He breathed hard, staring and moistening, as if reliving the devastating departure of the animal from his life, a departure whose traumatic nature was evidenced, obviously, not only by his remarks in this moment but by the fact that Dennis had never before mentioned the dog at all.

After a pause calculated to show respect, I said, "So when might it, the dog, possibly turn up, if ever?" and Den dropped his mug on his foot and elected to limp to a chair and recline with his head thrown back and his eyes closed and flickering. Now I definitely felt like needling him some more. But, to cast myself in a good light in my own eyes for future reference, I forebore.

A week later his former wife phoned again (her final call forever), and little shrieking sounds came from the phone before she hung up on him. Not a very evolved person, from the sound of it.

The next morning the bell rang. Raleigh was on the stoop.

He was tied to the iron banister, tangled in his leash, panting, smiling, and splashing spit around. I looked up the block, then down. Nobody. I ran to the corner, as though chasing a mugger. But she had mugged me and got away.

He appeared to be a sweet zany golden retriever, possibly with some overjuiced terrier stirred in. He was still pretty young — he had that young, eager, frisky, disorganized air.

Laying eyes on Raleigh, Dennis looked as though he might weep. "Oh, Raleigh, Raleigh boy! Raleigh boy! Raleigh boy! Raleigh boy! Raleigh Raleigh Raleigh, Raleigh boy, my Raleigh boy, my nice nice doggie boy!" and he hugged the dog's thick middle while the dog tried to whip around and nip him, and they struggled together for a long time, embracing on a stoop slick with drool. Raleigh wasn't tidy — some bits of hardened turds clung to his long butt fur. But he was handsome, with a broad, proud, oversized head. At last Den released his choke hold, we disentangled the dog and let him in, and, releasing a cloud of wet fur smell, Raleigh ran into the powder room and drank deeply from the toilet, then thundered up three flights to Den's study and urinated on the rug.

*

Within a week, tufts of gold fur were stirring in the hall-
ways like tumbleweed. Our clothes were hairy. Feeling
Raleigh in the house, Bianca seemed to tremble in her
basement pond. I began to share the care of Bianca now,
because Dennis had turned to his new love, his first. I
didn't really look at the frog; I just lifted the lid and
sprinkled, and flecks of fish meal, corn gluten, soybean
oil, and dried potato products floated down like the
beginnings of snow.

And who was Raleigh, the most beloved? He was a lost
dog, estranged from his ostensible breed. While most
retrievers are placid, Raleigh was freaked out. While most
retrievers are eager to please and quick to learn, Raleigh
could obey no commands at all. He had a temper so
unpredictable that he even surprised himself; he wasn't a
growler or a barker, but at random moments he'd threaten
to nip, so he had to be walked on an extremely short lead,
with his head choked up against Den's thigh. They'd
stroll down the block — Den blissful; Raleigh, tongue
lolling, yanked up against him; passersby confused.

Raleigh was like a mythological hybrid animal, half
something, half something else, raised in a fairy-tale
wood by a maniac. Raleigh knew a lot, but nothing useful. He could tell, for example, when the doorbell was
going to ring, and he would wake and run downstairs
and look at the chimes. When the bell rang a moment
later, he'd be as hysterically astounded and vindicated
as somebody winning the Publishers Clearing House
sweepstakes and would rush the door licking at his chest
and wheeling in circles, peeing.

He'd go into the back of a closet and wrestle out some fallen hangers, but if you threw a ball he couldn't find it, and if he found it he didn't bring it back. Raleigh didn't notice the cat! Raleigh wouldn't sit, stay, heel, or lie down. He didn't know when he was hungry. He wasn't sure when he had to go out. And still he never failed to anticipate the doorbell's chimes, on the basis of some subliminal airborne evidence, from rooms away, from day one. Raleigh our doggie boy was, it appeared, a sort of canine idiot savant, entirely conversant with irrelevancies.

Dennis was blind with happiness. "I love Raleigh. Don't you love Raleigh?"

"I like Raleigh," I said, telling my new husband my first big fat lie.

7

This period in our lives, which began so raggedly, soon turned silky. Months after his arrival, we would learn that Raleigh knew when Den and I were mad at each other — even silently angry, even angry unbeknownst to ourselves — and our animosity, however subterranean, hurt Raleigh's feelings. He'd watch us, hoping dog hopes. At first, though, in the early weeks of the dog's life with us, we weren't often mad — far from it; we were in a luminous honeymoon phase occasioned by Den's pleasure in Raleigh and Den's concomitant dreamy grateful honeyed niceness. Later we would discover some problems that couldn't be fixed by a pet — not by any of our pets, not by all of them combined. For now, it was dog and us.

While we made love, three heads on the pillows: mine, his, and Raleigh's. Or Dennis and I grappled like wrestlers while Raleigh circled the bed with a referee's intensity, his head in our armpits and between our thighs. Sometimes it was a long night for the dog: Den never pinned me and I never pinned him. Later on, unblinking, devoted, Raleigh would give my foot a lick, to spur me on.

Dennis had the delightful potency of a substantially younger man, and his lovemaking was vehement — meaty, zealous, headlong.

He was fearless. He'd cannonball from the doorway, stripping off his clothes. He'd jump right out of his shoes and land on the futon already rolling me with him, a Western hero; he didn't seem to realize he could get hurt. Urgent mood, brisk pace. We had sex like we meant it.

Den's touch was unusual — it hurt, but, upon reflection, nicely. I defend my husband: Yes he was rough but only out of enthusiasm. I enjoyed being pinched and scrubbed and tossed around by my hair! We'd wrestle and Dennis would clamp me in rocklike thighs.

A few times during our moist and fervid strivings, my husband fell out of the bed. Once, he bounced; but usually he'd land hard, chuckle philosophically, dive back in. I'd have to say our lovemaking was festive. But then I started to grow lonely in spite of the merriment, and perhaps, I'll never know, he did too — the way you both might, no matter how compatible you were, if, say, you always made love in total darkness.

*

Dennis was developing a habit: As wholehearted as he was in bed, there would nevertheless come a moment when, precipitantly, he'd bolt up and sprint away.

Was it me? Was it us? Was it a small amount of testosterone spiking, as it does in a youngish man every quarter hour or so, compelling him to rush into the savanna, kill wild animals, and drag them back to his encampment, or at least causing him (the way it routinely forces any ordinary joe, watching some tube with his wife, to rise from the couch, somnambulate to the kitchen, and stand gazing mystified into the refrigerator) to require a moment alone? (As we know, the chief determinant of my own contrasting need to keep Dennis near me in these moments was the oxytocin flooding my system, which hormone was also generating in me the helpless impulse, transitory but impressive, to bond, nest, bear young, read them *Story Number One,* buy them Ikea furniture, send them to Montessori school, teach them to use chopsticks at Phoenix Garden, and embark upon worrying about them steadily for twenty-five years as they strenuously bring themselves to the point where they bag graduate school to play in a band.)

Den just needed to go to the bathroom. He just needed to take some fluid out of himself or put some in, preferably both. There's no strangeness here, you will say. I said the same.

The first time it happened, I was lying twisted around him still trembling when, suddenly distracted, my husband peeled us apart, leaped up, and rushed away. How can I be a complainer? James Dean, Nijinsky, Omar

Sharif — these were surely never perfect lovers; I'm certainly not, myself. After Dennis's robust sensual generosity, his departure was, anybody can see, a small thing; still — it must be faced — it was a letdown. One night he exited the room so fast I saw his afterimage, glistening and pink.

That very night, Raleigh, fascinated, followed his master. I followed Raleigh. The hall was empty. On sections of bare floor, my feet left moist prints. Dennis had disappeared with the dexterity of a Hitchcock villain. When we found him he was standing dreamily in hard bathroom light, staring at the tile wall, consuming and discharging liquids simultaneously. In one big sad middle-aged hand was his penis, trickling into the bowl; in the other was a mason jar, from which he was drinking with a metronome's cadence, like a mechanical sipping bird.

Raleigh started barking. Bark bark bark. Bark.

Muttering from Den: "It's okay, boy. It's me."

Raleigh didn't believe him.

"Settle back, boy."

Bark bark. Barkbarkbark.

"Okay, boy. It's me, sweetie boy."

The dog backed up, stepped forward, backed up. Barkbarkbarkbark. Bark! Bark! Bark!

Den rolled his drowsy eyes and let them fall closed. He urinated. He dipped his head and sipped.

"Shut up, Raleigh," I said. I was still hormonally very pumped. I longed for and never wanted to see again

strange Dennis, who was compelled to abandon me —
us — in what was not yet the aftermath of our hours of
love. I turned and walked down the stairs, into the dark-
ened living room, across the carpet toward my favorite
piece of furniture, the pumpkin gold silk-velvet Victorian
daybed, whose curvaceous flank was gleaming metal-
lically in the darkness as street lamp light dropped in
stripes into the shadowy room. I gazed down at the
daybed as if at a reclining lover. I sat, thighs together so as
not to stain the expensive velvet. Fuck him and good-bye.

After a while, as I sat there calming down, feeling and
really appreciating the lovely silky fabric under my legs,
the upstairs grew quiet. Barking became dog coughs,
then Raleigh fell silent and I could hear his toenails
clicking, and then Dennis was walking around up there
slapping his bare feet. Hydrated and relieved, Den was
looking for me. Twice he called. I didn't answer. I leaned
against the daybed's solid back, and my hand hung
down and my fingers trailed as if in water, and my crav-
ings subsided as though forever, and my yearnings and
hatreds with them, while I listened to my husband's
footfalls above me as he searched, near the spot he had
left her, for his misplaced wife.

Day 94: Den and me, naked, holding hands. Raleigh.

Day 118: Me looking at Den. Den looking at watch.
Toothpaste on his chin.

Day 165: Den, very close in. Yelling. Forehead out of frame. Mouth dark and indistinct. Strange wet spot on face.

Day 166: A swath of out-of-focus rosiness: Den, forgetting to wait for the shot, briskly exiting (as during sex).

On Day 167 he knocked the tripod down.

We ate a large meal in which cheese figured prominently. Dennis, afterward on the chaise, a stranded odalisque, palpating his chest with busy fingertips: "I can feel my heart struggling."

"What? Your heart?"

"Heart, trying to push the blood through." He made ratchety choking sounds. Raleigh scrambled up and looked at him. "My veins, my —"

"*What is it?*"

"*Nothing.* Stop it. It's digestion."

The next morning he was a strangely pale and pensive Dennis.

"How are you feeling?" I inquired.

"Everything went down."

"So you feel okay? You look sort of funny."

"Fine. Great. Physically fine."

"So — what, then? Emotionally?"

Den, cheerfully, in the middle of the bedroom, wearing only a T-shirt, rampant. "I'm despondent."

"So how do you manage to be so exuberant?" I asked, genuinely curious.

"Circus genes."

Our second honeymoon drew to its close. Dennis's drastic physicality and the messes it made, and the fact, now emerging, that he could rarely do any ordinary thing in an ordinary way, and the tiresome predictability of all of this, and the fact that it was like this day after day, and my growing realization that it would always be this way and probably, as years passed, would worsen and then, as years passed, would become unbearable — well, I started to put in some time as that unloveliest and least-understood woman, a carper.

Den, for his part, was a counterpuncher. Game theory was alive for him. With each complaint of mine he'd turn his back and maintain a spirited muteness until he heard a silence to match his own. In rejoinder I'd berate the back of his shirt for longer than I would've addressed his face. He administered his sanctions swiftly and invariably, as game theorists and pet trainers tell us is the only way, and I upped the ante, and the battle was joined.

Arguably, the man was changed. I did think so. Dennis couldn't have been like this when I met him, nor when we married — wouldn't any sane woman have made note?

When we first sat at Lydia's holiday table, for example, didn't we dine normally, that is, in accordance with the twentieth-century American social norms probably elegantly explicated by redoubtable sociologist Goffman in one of his lesser-known tracts? Lydia is a woman of taste! This Dennis living in this house could not have been her guest! But forget the puzzle of the past: Now his dining habits had transmogrified.

The floor under his chair was thick with crumbs until Raleigh licked them; or the crumbs snowed down and the dog caught them on his tongue. For breakfast Dennis would buy a bagel across the street, carry it home half crushing it in his fist, tear it mangled from its small bag, lavishly butter it (glazing all his fingers), then hurl buttered bagel hunks in the direction of his face and pour mugs of milky coffee down his pants. At every meal Raleigh was feverishly watchful. Every time Den raised his fork, the dog's jaws anticipatorily snapped as though he were catching a bug.

"Do you think you may be developing an eyesight problem?" I asked, and my husband turned his back.

Is this what marriage is? Discoveries and discoveries, changes and changes, until everything you had is gone? Peeling some horrible onion rotting from the inside out? This couldn't be my Dennis! Some other Dennis had replaced mine! In a soap opera, after lengthy exposition it would've turned out that the man who ate breakfast this new way; who, when he made marinara sauce, splashed the walls so the kitchen looked as though something had been slaughtered there; whose trousers were speckled with cheese-morsel stains and drops of wine like blood spots — it would've turned out this guy was my guy's identical twin, returned from exile, bent on ruin, despairing and compulsive as a vampire and equally incapable of personal change. When I thought like this I felt half mystified, half bereft. I had the strong impulse to look in the sugar bowl and behind the doors for my own and former Dennis, as if he were some precious thing I couldn't find and feared might have been stolen.

And Bianca the frog in the basement would've been correct, had she been sentient, to fear him — he could've easily smashed into her bucket, knocked out the water, tipped her onto the floor, trod on her and crushed her and left her for dead. A squished pinkish-white smear. In fact, that the frog still survived under Den's aegis was one of a now proliferating number of mysteries. Consider the cat, originally Ginger Girl — after the accident, Icarus. She was our pet but we never saw her, except in flashes of furry orange as she ran to hide. But more about that later.

You will say I overvalued my spouse and, as people will at close range, ceded him too much of my power; or that, like Raleigh, I watched him way too hard. Or that I exaggerate. I am no exaggerator. No, my husband's new dishevelment was remarkable, potent, ramifying. It could destroy whole little worlds. Twice, other people's cars broke down when he drove them; their motors raced and they coughed and spiked fevers and suffered and clanked and stopped. His presence in a room could destabilize it — paintings shifted and books dropped off the shelves. Scissors rusted, glasses cracked, paint chipped, tires flattened, plants developed scale. One night we ate a beet puree, and afterward Dennis's napkin looked as though it had been used as a tourniquet.

I was as vigilant now as a new puppy owner. A day came when Dennis sat down with a snack and I whirled into the living room and spread newspapers under him. On that day, he stood, set down his Pepsi can and turkey club, removed his jeans, lifted his leg, and pissed on The Week in Review, Arts and Leisure, and the real estate section. The New York City rental market was continuing robust, I noticed under a puddle. In that moment we seemed exquisitely, perfectly mated, my husband and I. We smiled bitterly. "Very original," I told him. He told me, "Glad you think so."

But often enough we thought of ourselves as so many game and hopeful couples, accurately, will: not beginning to hate. Struggling with love.

We still had great moments. We'd get these connubial second winds. Dennis said I was a precious person, somebody amazing, like a combination of a diamond and a banana. He came up behind me and *gave me* a diamond and a banana. He felt my skull. "All those beautiful brains thinking those strange and beautiful thoughts," he said dreamily. He cupped his warm hands around my head and held on.

"Donald? Hi, it's me. Would you want to eat dinner at the Thai place with us tomorrow?"

"I can't tomorrow."

"Or Tuesday?"

Donald said, "Jeez. I'm so busy all this week. And next week is — hell too. Lemme see here. Jeez. No. I guess we better just, I don't know, wait and see how things go."

"Sallie? It's me. Dennis wants to take you and me out to dinner sometime this week. Call me back and tell my machine what night."

Eight days went by.

"Sal? It's me. I guess you must be away. Give me a call when you get this."

Three days went by. She left me a message: "Hi, it's Sallie. I'm sick as a dog. What a flu. You don't need to catch this one. I wouldn't even want to get together until I'm absolutely sure it's over."

Weeks later, an October night and Den and I in disputation. The phone rang; the machine picked it up. It was Sallie — she had never called back until now. We just let her talk on through our own raised voices. I did not at the moment want to hear whatever it was she thought.

Raleigh thundered down, doorbell chimed, we threw open the door. On the steps were bats and superheroes, behind them their pleasant, bored, devoted parents on the sidewalk under the stars. We gazed at these people. It was Halloween!

Is this how alone we are? Now united in embarrassment and guilt, Den and I rushed through our dim house throwing the lights on, looking for treats. "Wait wait!" we bellowed. Oh it's okay, the parents called, and they whispered to their children and turned to leave. *Wait!* we pleaded, and, what the hell, they waited. I ran back to make sure.

They were nervous; we could all hear Dennis and Raleigh smashing through the rooms, Den yanking open cabinets and scrabbling in drawers; this was precisely the sort of psychopaths' house the razor-blade-fearing parents had constantly in mind. The bats were growing fearful. They clustered closer together, black and jumpy. I pulled the children into the hall, cast them a big creepy smile, made them flap their wings. A larger, stoic but now very intimidated boy, wearing a fez, sacrificed himself to rescue the bats from my attentions: "I am Aladdin."

"And who is *this?*" I demanded jovially.

Whispering, near tears: "This is my brother."

At last, Raleigh wheeling and barking, Dennis rushed in to hurl quarters into the kids' plastic jack-o'-lantern buckets. The quarters hit with a clatter like sudden rain, and the children escaped, Den and I waving grandly as though from a considerable distance. We closed the door and turned off all the lights, and, alike in shame, waiting for the small voices to die down, sat together in the dark.

*

Soldiered on.

Since our first meeting at Lydia's on Horatio Street, a long and surprising year had gone by. For Thanksgiving, Dennis and I began hoping to be invited to Lydia's again. We wanted to sit at the table where we had met and repossess that old sanguine feeling. With each passing day we had a more intense, waiflike interest in being invited.

She did not invite us. When we phoned to drop hints she didn't return our calls.

We left messages for both Donald and Sallie, but they both had plans out of town. We called a few other friends, and they either didn't pick up or were too busy to talk.

And so it fell to Den and me to celebrate alone. We produced a feast: two Cornish hens, overcooked. Boiled paillard of chicken for Raleigh and the cat. For Bianca, dried brine shrimp and a guppy.

Dennis bashing through the swinging door, the platter tilting, the little hens sliding, Dennis crying, "Uh-oh! Uh-oh!"

I turned from lighting the candles to survey our holiday tableau. The pair of hens, napped with sauce, side by side on the rug; my husband astride them, a miserable giant, clutching parsley. He had butter on his face. He cast me a pleading look, and I left the room without a word.

8

New things began to happen. Just incidents, really, that ended in injury. Inside our renovated brownstone, we started to get hurt.

I was working on the computer (my parents' wedding pictures montaged with images of other couples), trying to learn to be clear and to not get lost. Meanwhile Dennis swung into a new mode: prodigies of composition. For six weeks he worked twelve hours a day like a real writer of novels, deep in the effort to create breathing and feeling characters, wandering the house possessed, a conduit for three hundred pages of the vast literature always waiting in the universe to be taken down, revised, corrected in page proof, published, remaindered, and stored in cardboard cartons in its authors' basements. He typed until his fingers swelled.

On his breaks, he tied plastic bags filled with ice chips around his hands, then shuffled upstairs and down, hearing the voice of his novel and dripping. "I'm awake but I'm dreaming," he said when we met in the hall.

"Should you slow down, Dennie?"

"Sweetheart, I can't."

On TV one night, a commercial featured Michael Jordan. "Look! You've gotta see him! Look at Michael!" With distended mitts he grabbed my head and swiveled it, and white pain flashed up the side of my neck. As I was the last person in America to find out, Michael's shoulders are unbelievably beautiful, and he can fly. To this day, years later, I can't quite turn my head.

Dennis stopped typing awhile and the edema left his hands. He held them up, admiring them, their basketball player's span, that one-and-a-half-octave spread. His wonderful big thick fingers removed my shirt, unhooked my bra, and got ahold of my nipples and rubbed them raw.

Dennis stepped on my foot. I can't prove he cracked a bone, but it anticipates weather and has never been the same.

Dennis went around into the garden and smoked a cigar. He flicked an ash, and it flew up inside his shorts and kissed his inner thigh with a big greasy burn.

Dennis entered the living room on a diagonal, a gorgeous hot flush already blooming in his cheeks.

"What, Dennie?"

"Wanta try something?"

"What?"

"I'm gonna show you."

"What is it?"

"Won't you just try it, sweetheart?"

"I don't know. Maybe. What is it?"

He cast me a soft look. Such tenderness, melting his face so that it sagged in unusual directions. In that moment he was an irresistible man, rosy and dewy and besotted. He said, "Just close your beautiful eyes."

When a moment later I peeked out, Dennis was sliding off his young-crocodile belt. (There were mysterious nicks in the belt, almost like a row of old scarred-over puncture wounds, as though the crocodile baby had, preparatory to being sliced into expensive leather goods, turned around over its own shoulder and repeatedly nipped its own flank.)

"I'm looking," I told him. "I don't want to miss this."

Dennis's foggy breath on my ear cartilage, his special goofy Casanova grin. I grinned too, with girly curiosity, and held out my wrists to be cuffed. But he stepped behind me to tug my arms back and belted them behind my back. A one-second thrill of claustrophobia and then I felt fine. He unzipped our trousers and took a long time wiggling them off. He sat me, his willing captive already thoroughly in the grip of Stockholm syndrome, onto the daybed, my bare buttocks eagerly touching the velvet, my dark eyes meeting his. I was now wearing only a pink sweatshirt, two sheer black knee-highs, and, as I say, his belt. (My thighs were remarkably white and large. I was almost alarmed by these two wide shivering animate things, but then, in a be-here-now spirit, I took note and let them go.) Dennis's own powerful bottom half appeared, somewhat ruddy below his Armani shirt, and his favorite tie (parti-colored frogs on a black Italian-silk ground — record-breaking Manhattan neck-wear seller of 1986) swung between us. His engorged penis bounced slightly, then disappeared as his shirt draped cowl-like over it.

Unclear how this was going to work — I was sitting awfully low, and wasn't he getting into too deep a crouch? Nevertheless, I spread my thighs to receive the organ of my beshirted lover. Opposite me, on the edge of the coffee table, Dennis was taking a seat.

Have I mentioned that the tabletop was glass? "Den, don't put your weight on —"

An immense sound, exactly like an explosion — the crack, the whoosh, the vibration in the walls — and the table split and he plummeted. Daggers flew up and he landed in shards. Blood. It spurted from somewhere — from him, from his lower half! — and his face turned very white and stupid.

"Oh, Dennis! Oh! — *is it your balls?*" He lifted the hem of his shirt and looked down at his genitals, which were sticky. Blood everywhere, in pools and splatters, like a cop show set in horrible mythic New York City and Dennis the DOA.

You know so well: sodden carpet, red footprints, then the naked man supine in the bottom of the bathtub, sweat droplets on his too-white brow, his paw over his eyes. All that streaming crimson against the pearly porcelain. We iced his ankle, we got it stopped, it took hours, he fainted and lolled in the redness — oh, I can't be bothered to flesh it all out!

Let it go. The daybed had to be reupholstered. We threw out the rug.

After a week of tremulousness, Den recovered and relaxed his work schedule and took himself off to kick Pudney's butt.

Pudney, a wan, intelligent fellow, played only the American game — smaller court and faster ball. On the other hand, Pudney was the one remaining local squash player willing to get on a court with Dennis. Other players, Pellegrino drinkers and nervous nellies, had one by one fallen away; Pud was not overfussy. Now, a scant hour after Den's departure from the house, Pudney phoned from the emergency room and suggested I meet him there. It was not serious. "But it is messy," he told me, superfluously.

When I arrived, Pudney was pacing outside; he appeared to be taking some kind of walking cure, maintaining a constant rhythm as if to march himself into steadiness. He had been nauseated by all he had seen. Den was far more accustomed to squash on a European court — today, on the narrower American court, way too cramped for Dennis, he had reached for a shot and bashed his head into a wall.

Inside, my husband was manic, bouncing in a molded plastic chair, talking jovially while stanching his wound with lively fingers. Blood had pooled on his shoulder and splashed down his T-shirt, dripped onto his shorts, splotched his bare knees, speckled his shoes. He appeared to have stood under a burgundy-colored waterfall. *"Hi,"* he said, grinning crazily.

He was pale but galvanized, on a talking jag. He gestured expansively with wet red hands, with a completely inappropriate air of being eager to help out. Except that he was slathered in his own blood, he seemed less like a prospective patient than a strangely sociable emergency room doc, a trauma cowboy medicating his own depression by rising to the occasion. Other emergency room visitors, under the weather though they felt, were gazing at him impressed. It was not a good sign: Smashing himself in the head, Dennis had come alive.

Eight stitches. And Pud wouldn't play anymore. In fact, not one month later, Pudney moved away.

And a week later: Dennis had borrowed my keys, the doorbell had (this worried me) fallen mute, and when I arrived home after doing errands Den couldn't hear my knock from his study, where he was barreling back and forth composing sentences to the accompaniment of

Miles and Cannonball Adderley, "One for Daddy-O." I went across to the bagel place to phone him, but the machine was picking up our calls. Several times I climbed the front steps and approached our door, hoping Raleigh would sense my intention to ring the bell, but it didn't work.

I was locked out.

In brilliant light and unseasonably warm winter air, I sat down on the *Village Voice* on the stoop. The neighbor boy was on the next-door stoop with a T-shirt draped on his head, snuggling there as if cozily. It was quite nice here in this unaccustomed silence. When the sun dropped behind the bagel shop, I covered myself with leaves of newspaper to maintain body heat in case there was a long haul to come. I was not unaccompanied. As I say, I had the neighbor boy, a depressed boy to be sure and variously punctured with silver rings, but still a sort of companion. I had my Leica, my little pal, and through its clever retina I looked around the neighborhood. After a while I started shooting the houses of the neighbors across the street with a long lens, trying to push past their French lace curtains, penetrate their careful casual drawing rooms, send my eye back into their pantries where they stored their jarred artichokes, sun-dried tomatoes, Evian and Mueslix, enter their calm and comprehensible lives. What a strange serene interlude. I didn't stop taking pictures of that distant world until my six rolls of film ran out. Eventually Dennis would emerge.

And here's what I found out, as — like a child who has threatened to run away, and whose mother has called her bluff and packed her suitcase — I sat there in zazen blankness on the top step of my own house: I had nowhere else to go.

But what was this? Not an injury. Just a moment.

9

The housekeeper quit. Luz would be flying to visit her mom in Guatemala. "And when I return in United States?"

Me, eagerly: "Yes? When will that be?"

"No more working."

"No more working?"

"I'm sorry."

"No more working here?"

She pressed on me a beautiful gaze of fervent sympathy.

"You can't work for us anymore?"

"I'm sorry. I cannot work."

A devastating blow! I was reeling! Hang the expense, what was money to us, I had to get her back! "If it's your salary, I could definitely improve your —"

"Mrs., the salary is so good. No problem with salary."

"But Luz, you've been crucial help, why do you have to — is there a reason you can tell me?"

She hesitated a long, oddly embarrassing time. She pulled a handkerchief from her pocket and wrung its neck. "See, there is a problem?"

And suddenly I wanted to help us through this moment, to prevent its contamination by undue candor. With a big fat contorted empathic look on my face, I cleverly asked, "Is your problem . . . personal?"

She blushed with gratitude and relief. "Yes! Personal problem!"

"I hope it's not serious."

"Serious, no," she affirmed.

"Gee, we really could use help with all the cleaning," I observed with dignified understatement.

She looked away, to give me a private moment naked, needful, and alone.

"Well, is there anyone else you could recommend?"

"I cannot recommend," our fleeing housekeeper said mournfully, and, two tactful ladies, Luz and I gave it a rest.

Having made our messy bed, Dennis and I were being left to lie in it with our dog. *You scared the housekeeper away.* But I didn't say that — only in my dreams.

What's the big deal? Hundreds of millions do fine without household help. (Anyway, we could find another helper, I thought without hope.) We were just one couple and three nice pets. We were just one married couple in one house in a country filled with houses and apartments and mobile homes containing the married living equally successfully with and without housekeepers as far as the eye could see and way beyond. And the divorced, you will say, and the homosexual. And the people who eat without splashing.

Our first winter was passing fast.

A day came when I noticed our life had become an alarming thing. Now my heart rate was elevated with regularity, and anything, anything — yellow grains of English muffin dust on the counter — frightened me or pitched me into a rage. I'd tremble and my heart would jump in my chest.

A black ball of sock under a chair.

The cold coffee grounds in the paper filter, drying, stiffening.

I would twitch with fury, breathe deep breaths. My struggle for equanimity consumed long hours.

10

The last week of April, one year into our union, found Dennis and me in his mother's garden in Carmel Valley, breathing California air, studying detachment and trying to fix our hearts. Like me, Dennis was, as I've said, an only child. Today, after flying across the country for his mom's birthday, deftly avoiding death by airplane, we were not permitted to lift or carry anything, or to move at all. Our job was to reaffirm that we were still and always children. We sat.

Every small anniversary, now, was like this: I would recall our shared pleasure and hopefulness on this date one short year before. Now I remembered our last April 27, not long before our wedding.

We had spent that Sunday with Donald and some pleasant silent woman he was dating, in steeply mounting summerlike heat in the Brooklyn botanical garden — Shakespeare's herbs and baby waterfalls, lilacs — among thousands of Chinese Americans, Japanese Americans, Italian Americans, Turkish Americans, Armenian Americans, Irish Americans, African Americans, Latin Americans, Hasidic Americans, and a few post-hippie lapsed Episcopalians. We were two pairs of assimilated but culturally Jewish Americans, enjoying our home borough, until Dennis backed into an entire Korean American wedding party and knocked down a glittering, flowerlike, utterly young bride, who fell and from the pavement immediately tried to trip him with her bead-encrusted white satin toe.

That was unfortunate, the girl-bride sullied and enraged in the dust. Her brothers offered to beat up Dennis, then changed their minds, straightened their tuxedo jackets, turned their impressive backs. True, it was additionally hectic since Donald and the girlfriend almost in that precise moment recalled a previous commitment and were forced to hastily cut our visit short. I do clearly remember Dennis and me stepping quickly away ourselves from the infuriated wedding party, both of us still optimistic and expansive, like the untroubled lovers we were then.

Now, in the garden in Carmel Valley, we sat in unpainted Adirondack chairs. Den's mom, Rochelle, had bought the chairs for their piney, Eastern smell — if we pressed our noses to them, she said, we'd smell a pine woods. Trapped, Den and I sniffed the armrests; left behind on his was a wet spot where Den's nose had been, as though Raleigh had nuzzled it. I admit now that when I saw the wet spot I kind of wanted to knock my husband down. I photographed the wetness.

He said, "What's the subject of the picture?"

I played deaf.

He poked my shoulder, my heart jumped, and we burst into flame. *"What's the picture?"*

Quietly and fast, I said it was a shot of his armrest, one shot, and in any case I didn't like his tone and didn't like his attitude and didn't want my shoulder bruised and frankly didn't feel like sustaining any further injury right now of any kind, I was a photographer and I was planning to continue taking photographs regardless of whatever lather he had managed to work himself into for whatever reason known only to him.

Panting, I gazed all around. The garden was stuffed with sweet peas, breath-of-heaven, and tree roses, all blooming. The breeze picked up, and a little lemon tree shivered. I sighted through the viewfinder. In the corner of the frame, Rochelle's white cat planted its two front feet on a tiny lizard's tail, then bit off its head.

He poked me again.

When I turned, he was looking away.

I returned to the garden through my long lens.

He said: "You're making me look like a bad person."

"No. I'm not. What I did was take a picture."

"No. You're telling *bad stories* about me."

"In fact, it's not a story. It's actually a representation of an object."

"It's an *'object'*? It's *'an object'*? Are you for real?"

"What the hell is your point?" I said. "Is it the case that all of a sudden you don't know what a photograph is? It's an image! It's about interpretation! It's about —"

"No!" He flushed, fast. He had something, it would turn out, extremely reasonable to say. "This is bullshit of the usual stripe! This is another story you're telling! Making a story is just selecting what to *advert to!* That's all it is! And you're telling a story all the time! And you're telling a story every day! And the story *you particularly have selected to tell,* and the story *you keep telling,* every goddamn day, no matter what I try to do, is a crummy, lousy, creepy, damning, mean-spirited story *about what a complete jerk I am!"*

I snapped his picture, he swatted at the camera, I ducked out of range. This is what we had become.

A long time later, the silence was broken by Rochelle, Dennis's mother, staggering from the house under a platter of foods. Dennis stood, looked fiercely genial, and tried to wrestle the platter from his mother's grip, almost knocking her down, and some chicken legs bounced into the grass, and, wildly irritated, she kicked at them, and I took a shot of him and her grappling together, while she slapped at Den until he lost his balance and fell back into his chair. Without a word, Rochelle kicked the chicken legs into a greasy heap in the grass. She wheeled and jogged back to the house.

As inevitable as Rochelle's ferocity must have been, it shocked me. She was his mom! She usually described the boy-Dennis with ordinary stubborn devoted-mother fondness. In her story, he was — always would be — an odd but delicious little child, worried and pink haired and nutty. Now I recalled she claimed she had toilet trained him at six months, defeating all records, only to have him relapse, sweetly, implacably, into an untrained state that lasted until he was nearly five.

In their summer house on the screened porch in 1956, she had told me, she would set the plump long-lashed two-year-old guy into his high chair and then phone the neighbors, single women and childless couples and lonesome grandparents, who would come right over to watch him eat. Every time baby Dennis gurgled and patted cottage cheese into his curls, the neighbors applauded.

Early summer evenings during Eisenhower, still bright out. A monster being made.

No, I thought, I'm a monster myself, totting up a human being's sins. He's a good man and does not deserve to be represented by the list I'm keeping. I fall asleep at night adding to his permanent record; in the morning I wake, see drool on his pillow, and begin again.

Twenty minutes east of us, gray whales steamed northward through the Pacific, spouting like fountains. They traveled in pods, real families. Den and I had been sitting so long and artificially that we were becoming agitated convalescents — feverish, dazzled, weak. My nose was running and I wiped it. My pulse began to settle. After all, Den, as it happened, had a large and shapely cock. In the confinement of my piney chair, I began to pass some time thinking about his penis's excellent hydraulics, its unusually dependable lifting and hardness, and its thickness, and its temperature which was delectably hot. An organ like this was a physical reality like sky and water, something the most distracted, even deranged, person couldn't mess up.

I glanced at him — his hair was tangled and he looked lost and sweet. Even now there might be the construction of a shared m.o.

"I would like to make love with you," I whispered, and, with a suddenly gorgeously happy face, he squeezed my wrist so hard that my mind blanked and white sparks drifted in the fragrant air.

Later, exhausted, in our bed in the crypt-cold stuccoed guest room of Rochelle's adobe-post house, we were lying close. My husband whispered to me: "I didn't marry you to be photographed. I didn't marry you to be told what I have become. I married you for us to love each other."

As we've heard, frogs in a pan of steadily heating water will not notice when the environment begins to boil. All the way home on the plane we sat in separate rows and thought hard. Back in Brooklyn, responsible tenacious married people after all, we rededicated ourselves. We declared ourselves jointly and equally at fault. We scheduled some talks. I talked while he listened; the timer clanged; he talked while I listened.

Out of our discussions emerged a shared belief that together, and lamentably early in the game, we two had been neglecting the important work that all marriages require if they are to continue to grow. Must do more

things together. Share hobbies. Meet others. Turn out-
ward side by side.

That's how Den and I, only occasional wine drinkers,
started frequenting bars. Together, of a late afternoon,
our steps quickening, we'd accompany each other down
the sidewalk to the Spanish place or the Middle Eastern
place and lash Raleigh to a meter, in a hurry to be sitting
in cool interior darkness alongside other disappointed,
vacillating human beings. Inside these modest taverns,
the way you will when you're alone, we watched people.
Each of us did it surreptitiously, trying not to hurt the
other's feelings; but we needed to learn how people live.

At the bar we'd order many tumblers of seltzer, the
occasional glass of perfumey chardonnay. In concert,
and as if fortuitously, we'd strike up (or, as the weeks
went on, resume) conversations with other patrons.
Now Den and I found we were excellent companions to
those we did not know — interested yet unintrusive,
pleasant yet self-contained, empathic without being too
lugubrious, vivacious without getting too wild. People
on the contiguous stools would confide in us, and after a
while I'd sometimes ask to take a picture. Somebody
who would immediately recount a story hair-raising in
its personal detail, casting back to harrowing days,
bringing the anonymous listener up to the freighted present with all its failure and loss and regret and shame —
that same raconteur was almost never prepared to have a
picture taken. This surprised me, but — as wouldn't any
photographer, or am I wrong? — I persevered. Anyway,
by the time I asked, the storyteller and I were barstool

intimates with that barstool obligation to one another: My subject would usually plod out into late-afternoon sun and placidly squint at the camera, and I would take a tactful single shot. Implicit in this transaction was our shared intention, never to be tested, to save each other's lives.

Evening after evening, on seats patched with duct tape, in smoke and dusky light, Dennis and I became popular. Out here among the public, I couldn't help noticing, Den lifted his glass meticulously and sipped without incident; for my part, I was unvigilant, calm. Out here, we were transformed. As lonely as alcoholics, we consumed only polite sips of wine, so we didn't produce temper, overeagerness, sulking, or tears. He and I had, I think — and continued to develop in those weeks while outside the summer ripened and we lived at the bar rail as our alternate selves — a look about us of what I'd have to call readiness. People could see it. They would ask us if we were traveling. They were close; we were searching.

But searching for what? Eager to discover, if we could (although it would soon become clear that we two, together, could not), what others knew. We were ready if necessary to do Heimlich. Ready if necessary to dance all night.

My nipples. His penis. Many glistening individual hairs. Wet sounds in the room.

We still made love. Of course we did. I enjoyed amnesia (probably, I now think, he did too): I always set out with voluptuous pleasure, unaware that our voluptuousness was going to end precipitately with me feeling I'd been lifted, swooped around, and dropped off a cliff. The cutting short of it was growing drastic. His exiting for the drink and the bathroom was happening earlier every time.

I started counting.

I came three times, he came, and we lay a moment entwined. I was starting again to move under him when thirst assaulted my husband and he jumped up and left.

Or I came twice, he came, and we lay a moment gasping as if washed up on some shore, and he had to pee.

Soon, I could come once, or sometimes not. Even to mention this reveals me as compulsive, ungrateful, overdemanding, as Dennis pointed out. But fuck it. So be it. We were always out of time.

Sweaty and flirty, I'd try to tease him into staying awhile, but he'd grow alarmed and unwind my playful strangling arms. Stay, stay a minute! *Thirsty. Gotta drain the snake.* Was this a problem? Was it a sexual problem? It was not a problem you could tell anybody about, had we had anyone left to tell. Still, it worsened.

At last we talked. Den explained to me that lovemaking was various, there was no reason it was required to be always the same, that women sometimes came a lot and sometimes not at all, there was no impotence here nor prematurity here nor god knew even the slightest

lack of attention to the needs and desires of one's partner, didn't we make love for two hours sometimes, and,
in short, couldn't we leave a good and pleasurable thing
well enough alone.

"Never two hours. Not anymore. Nowhere near."

"Oh you're quite wrong." He cited a time we had lav-
ished three, and he was correct.

"We agreed we should talk more about things," I said.

"Areas of differing perspectives," he said. "Absolutely,
honey."

I said, "Well, we sort of stop before it's over."

"No, sweetheart," he said tenderly. "That is not true."

"It sort of is, to me."

"Tell me about it."

"Well, before it's over, we —"

"I have to interject something here at the outset. In no
way do we stop before it's over. When it's over, sometimes I get thirsty. I go get a drink of water. That's, I have
to say, the true extent of your grievance."

"I'm not complaining," I said. "I'm beyond complaining. It's at the point where I'm kind of wondering —"

" 'Beyond complaining,' " he said.

"I mean, why *do* we stop so fast?"

Dennis said: "We don't stop fast. That is a figment of
your imagination, honey. For some reason I don't know
anything about, your imagination is casting around for
more things to resent about me, and that's what it came
up with — 'we stop fast.' We don't stop fast. We don't
stop fast. We go on and on, as you would not deny, and

frankly it's sometimes *almost entirely in the service of your enjoyment.*"

"I don't mean it's short," I said doggedly. "I meant the end part is sudden. It's a bit of a shock."

He looked sad for both of us. "Things do end."

"Well, sure, but —"

"Things come to a close," he said. "At which point you've developed the habit of recoiling as if I have punched that sweet little nose."

"I'm not saying you're not a good lover. I'm saying we sort of stop short. I'm *wondering* about it."

"Your wondering is taking the form of complaining about me and I don't think that's warranted and I think it's perverse. I think we make love for a normal time, *longer* than normal, we enjoy it, and a lot of it is for your satisfaction. I'm attentive, I know you would not deny that. I want to be positive that you come, and you *do* come, and frankly I think you're just mad at me about something else and what the hell is it? What the hell is it? What the hell is it? What the hell could it be?"

Beside me on the chair was my Leica. I picked it up and I started shooting. His face turning, swinging back, glaring (three shots). His torso as he stood, his body moving forward, wallpaper behind — the camera faintly clicked as he lunged toward me across the rug. The room seemed to be fluttering and whirring, his arm came into the frame, and he grabbed at me and I stopped and set the camera down.

He was standing above me, enraged. I smiled up.

He said, "I don't know what you're up to, lady, but I can tell you I ain't impressed."

I said: "You can admit it or you can deny it. But we do stop making love very suddenly, and it's weird."

Dennis said: "No. We do not."

At last a day arrived when we were making love and Den pulled out while he himself was still coming. He leaped up and staggered, bobbling and spurting, toward the door. I rushed after him. I smacked his damp shoulder, spun him around, and tried to smother him with a pillow.

That devil! Because he was standing when I pressed the pillow against his face, he just stepped neatly backward, landing against the bedroom wall as if thrown there, his stiff bouncy penis already beginning to droop. Semen dripped down his thigh. He said, "So where's your camera when you need it?"

Absolutely right, Dennis. The picture I would've shot: my enemy, genitals pendent, back to the wall.

11

But, as I continue to say, you know how marriage is. Deaths and resurrections. Just when it seemed impossible, we planned a romantic evening.

Anticipatorily, my husband staggered into the living room Bunyanlike under a heap of logs, knocked the mail off the table, stomped on the envelopes and slipped to one knee, bellowed ("Ow ow! Ow!"), and unloaded with a sound like an avalanche. Foreplay, I thought unworthily. Later, he and I struggled together half the night, naked all over the rug, expressing ourselves. I was resigned and enthusiastic, as uninhibited as though this were my last day on earth, because, after all, who would notice? (One of the several good things about lovemaking with Dennis: I enjoyed the privacy.) Blind and impervious, in flickering firelight, for hours we swam through hot spots and cold as through a deep pool. At intervals Den would leap up — naked, naturally, and wet — to hurl logs in, stab at the blaze like a maniac with a bayonet, jump back, slap the screen on, fall again onto our floor-bed already grunting with passion. Showers of sparks. Above us lay dreamy Raleigh on the newly reupholstered velvet daybed, whistling in his sleep.

Near dawn, dear Raleigh shuddered and nearly woke. My eyes fell open. Dennis and I were lying where something titanic — some hope, some fear — had thrown us onto the kilim. We lay in cold semen seepings, tangled in quilts, in the postures of car crash victims. In fact, viewed in its entirety, the scene looked not so much like the aftermath of romance as the remains of a hit-and-run. There was debris — kindling, matches, tongs and bellows, balls of newspaper, pressed-sawdust logs suffused with lighter fluid, drained and tipped-over claret glasses, half-empty cognac glasses, quarters and dimes, our watches and jeans and underwear and shoes. In some final or penultimate agony, Den had rolled about on a tube of K-Y jelly, and glistening around us on the polished floor were K-Y islands, transparent blobs thick with dog hair and twigs.

His familiar scent, approximately trebled in intensity, was thick on my skin; I shifted and a rich smell rose, telling our whole night's story. I lay still and took a look at us, prostrate (him) and supine (me). Yes, our limbs were splayed and broken. All we needed were chalk marks around us. Spent Dennis, one of the world's noisiest, ruddiest, busiest men, was too quiet, too white, too still. Lying in half-light in creepy morning silence, on a cold floor splotched with jelly, beside a fireplace stuffed

with ashes, I saw after a while that I was imagining —
idly but fully and in exhaustive naturalistic detail —
something unimaginable: my beloved husband dead.

I see how the language of armed conflict insinuates itself
into even the most pacific sections of the narrative. That
noon, at breakfast:

"Bombshell night, huh?"

"It was great, Den."

He rushed to the closet and back again: "Check this
out, honey! I bought you a better slide projector!"

"Oh thank you, what a nice —"

He dropped it on Raleigh, who jumped a foot, and I
sprang up as if reaching for my sword.

We had made it through a winter and deep spring was
arrived. Several times a day now I climbed up from my
basement darkroom and stepped around to the garden
to watch the clubs flying in brilliant May air: the neighbor boy was juggling. The adopted child of the Doctors
Rolfe, two excellent Jungians (inordinately celebrated,
as tall people so often are), he had recently flunked out
of freshman year at Middlebury; entirely without information about the rest of his life, the little pierced and
bleached and morbid guy spent half the day biting his
fingers on the stoop with his T-shirt on his head and the
other half throwing the clubs. From my vantage point
next door I could feel his anxiety settle right down every

time he got the clubs moving. Psychically out of balance
because temporarily lost in the world, he was nevertheless simultaneously an elegant juggler whose artistry
spoke of perfect equipoise: the kid was good. I couldn't
see him — I had never seen him standing up — but I
didn't need to: I saw the clubs. They flipped up and
they dropped, whirling for hours behind the brick wall
and locust trees that separated the lad's world from
mine.

One day I called quietly to him. "Wesley? Wesley?
Wes?" But he didn't hear me, and I didn't raise my
voice. Frankly, my feeling was, we were as one: me lurking behind expensive plantings, and the shrinks' son
whose unseen hands made those clubs, over and over,
rise and snap into place. Each of us daily more alone
with the problem, like a person going deaf.

Walking past the butcher shop, I saw my husband
inside. He was leaning forward across the counter, and
the butcher was setting a bite of meat into his mouth.

Dennis owned a fifteen-year-old Alfa, a bruiser with
cracked leather seats, which was parked under a tarp
in the alley alongside our house, in an indentation in
our garden wall, safe from view. I started driving it.
I started taking it out early and late, when traffic was
light. I would climb in, back it whining into the street,
accelerate down the block, run it up out of the sluggish

low gears, punch in the Pops Staples tape, and start to cry.

The songs; and the amorphous sexiness of the over-experienced, diminished but still potent machine; and being in an enclosed and private space; and not being able to attend to anything else except the road; and having a limit on the time I'd be inside the car, so that anything I did here, no matter how compelling, couldn't take on a life and continue forever — it was these factors that seemed to release me into welling tears and sometimes truly abandoned weeping. Backing out of the alley, checking the mirror, hearing the garbage trucks and dawn sounds of the city around me, before I could identify any thought I'd already be misty and snuffly, with a terrible thickness developing in my chest. I was trapped in this alien person I had become, somebody poised to strike and full of not knowing.

I had to drive to Princeton to shoot a writer. I backed out the Alfa. At eight in the morning, the Belt Parkway was overheating beside that sweep of calm sea, silver blue with a glaze on it. I swooped across the Verazzano into complicated New Jersey, over water, through sky, sobbing like a widow. At the tollbooth, I grabbed my ticket, and the toll taker cried, "Don't snatch!" Down the turnpike as fast as I dared, rushing toward a bright sky resting on the horizon under its roof of smog.

Blowing my nose, I started racing a red Thunderbird. (It was only in the high gears that the Alfa could race;

though Den wouldn't admit it, the car was slow off the light; Dennis pretended it sat day and night under its stiffening tarp just waiting to mop up everything below a Maserati.) After I passed him, the T-bird man looked, in the mirror, reposeful, comfortable with his own wide shoulders and expressive hair. He blew by in the left lane, and I took a shot of his taillights. Then an invisible thread began to form, linking him and me. Like a long-married couple executing their practiced samba, we didn't have to look at each other to move in concert, and we bent to each other's rhythm and leapfrogged smoothly and fast, never encountering a cop, so that by the time I turned off at exit nine I had passed his car twenty-five times and submitted twenty-six times to his passing mine, and as we tapped our horns in salute I already missed him.

Of course what he and I had actually been doing wasn't racing, but keeping company. Talking about what it means to stay side by side.

Down in Princeton, spring had come violently. I drove straight into some moist and flowery element: pink trees, perfumed air. Hundreds of men and women and boys guiding their roaring machines, shearing the carpets of green.

I parked in front of the writer's place in a neighborhood of porches and Big Wheels, where he was renting from a young family. As I approached his separate entrance he emerged, rushing forward. He was a giant-sized little boy, dark and full lipped, with long eyelashes shading true pink cheeks; he was moving toward me down the walk, fingers trailing along the side of the house, while I took his picture, and he smiled and bowed. It soon became clear he was willing to pose for long hours, with any props, in any place; he was an entirely cooperative subject, whose agreeableness turned out to be his only flaw — he rarely stopped smiling. Most of his short stories took place in lavatories. Now, inside his apartment of two dark, morbidly suburban rooms, he sat for the camera flanked by toilet and hamper, grinning like a fiend.

The writer told me that at night, lying on his cot inside his tiny high-ceilinged bedroom, he repeatedly imagined expanding the space by turning the room on its side. He boiled water on a hot plate and brewed green tea. He bent to pour and was made happy by his own curls falling into his own bright eyes (that's the shot I kept for myself — his bent head). He danced me across the lawn, admired the Alfa, tucked me in, and said such a sweet farewell that I suddenly felt connected and calm and optimistic — I felt, in other words, okay, all the way down the block.

Around town, self-possessed little children were walking home from school, close to the sidewalk and the drifts of petals where the trees meet the ground, down where they live their lives at the bottom of the frame.

I loved the crossing guard! Mine was the first car in line, and she had me wait a long time while other cars slowed behind me. I could see she was authoritarian, a player of favorites, but I loved her with a dizzying, fast-ripening love. I loved her high-tops, her short muscled calves, the orange apron embracing her fireplug torso, her economical bossy gestures. With the small children she was deliciously patient and sweet; with everybody else, despotic. I leaned out to take her picture and she threw me a vicious glance. Of course I shot it anyway, and she turned her head and I got a blur of arms and hair.

And so I peopled my day with subjects whose images I actually didn't quite get, who will certainly never know each other, whom I will certainly never see again. I matted them together. It's a triptych:

The fancy brake lights of a Thunderbird exiting my life.

A crossing guard, turning away.

The crown of curls of a boy made mysteriously happy simply by being himself.

On the way home I went the long way in order to take a few pictures of beautiful toxic industrial North Jersey — the steel skywalker animals stalking across Kearny, clusters of lights glittering all day in false dusk, refineries with their eternal flames. Well, you know why I chose this detour, out of loneliness.

12

In loneliness, as we know, anyone who cares for you can become the object of a kind of vagrant love: dry cleaner, hair cutter, naturally any masseuse if you visit one; occasionally the doctor; always the nurse. If any of these evinces a bad attitude you can be crushed like a pip. Otherwise, depths of gratitude. The guy who fixes the frame of your eyeglasses (which you will have broken yourself, when you're lonely, by some method like forgetting they're in bed with you and fitfully rolling back and forth and crushing them in the night), this wonderful simple calm optician, holding up your glasses in delicate fingers, gazing at the glasses to see what's wrong, reconstituting them easily with tiny tools, rolling in close on his rolling chair, fluently setting the glasses straight back onto your face — he's your beloved. His fingertips graze the hair above your ears, and all week those follicles hark back to that fastidious touch.

First I'd known myself to be autonomous, then self-sufficient, then solitary; then, suddenly, lonely as a bug. Again it occurs to me now — too late — that Dennis was too. I think you approach this condition as if across an expanse of dark water. You head toward it for a long time, seeing only its outlines ahead, and arrive suddenly, like a speedboat crashing into a dock.

As affluent lonely people will, I made appointments for various checkups.

My periodontist, Heshy, was a spiritual leader. He talked like one, he looked like one: the religious man's calm, of course; the dispassionate acceptance of human folly; the philosophical constancy — that air of proceeding cheerfully in the face of despair; and true wispy blondness. He was the kindest person I have ever known. He berated no one for neglecting to floss, only smiled with his eyes closed.

Well, loneliness called me to his office. I rose early, arrayed myself fastidiously, flew through the streets. Outside Heshy's I stopped awhile, watching patients emerge, locate a reflecting surface, and bare their teeth. Very few experiences in my recent life had seemed to warrant enhancement; but now, on Heshy's molar-shaped doormat, I rolled a joint and smoked it.

Inside, the waiting room was not cold but precisely cool, perfect, like a drink from a spring, spongy underfoot as a forest floor, hushed as the nondenominational cathedral it was. The waiting room was empty today and the furniture floated in a mauvey light.

Receptionist: "Be right with you? You okay?"

Me (first spoken words today, in economical response to both questions): "Absolutely no problem."

On the walls, signs spoke of keeping perspective and doing your best and reaching toward the light and trying and trying again, about charity, amity, life's brevity, hope. Bach was somewhere — actually, at this large and resonant moment, everywhere. I slumped deep in the cushions of a velour sectional, feeling completely comfy and humming along.

After liquid hours in the waiting room, I found myself in the inner office, reclining in a bedlike chair, with a reinforced-paper bib clipped on my shirt, listening to the tiny round sink swirling its water with a sound like a rill in a glade. Then, with a Q-Tip, Sharon was applying topical anesthesia — piña colada flavor, pineapple-dominated. Then Sharon ran in and out and in and out, and some x-raying both went on forever and rushed by, and after it was over the numbing finally kicked in, but I didn't tell Sharon, to spare her feelings, and then Heshy was somehow in the room, and I was shaking his strange rubbery hand, which turned out to have his latex glove on it, and he was acting as though that were completely normal, to shake that way, not shrinking back but giving me a firm, confiding, exceedingly lengthy shake. He exhibited my X rays, depicting the ghostly teeth. I was alarmed by the length of the roots but then I went into a dream from which I immediately emerged hearing Heshy say, "Congratulations. Those are nice long roots you have."

Heshy was worried about my wear patterns and told me about a thirty-five-year-old man he had been following for twenty years, whose teeth were worn down to nubs, which story caused me to look concerned and then laugh inappropriately. I was remarkably stoned. After a while Heshy was somehow, sadly, gone, and then I was at the receptionist's desk. With a little thrill of virtue, I offered to pay cash now in order to sustain a five-dollar reduction of my bill. Importantly, I noted the amount in my checkbook, with an air of being the sort of person who keeps meticulous records. The receptionist eyed me and I cut her dead. All this must've been only a distraction from my confounding life back at the house with Dennis, but at the moment I was heartbroken to be leaving this temple of Heshy's loving-kindness, and I impulsively turned and rushed back into the inner offices and, encountering Heshy in the hall, I embraced him, crushing him and his lab coat and all his accepting forgiving mildness and another patient's X rays to my now pained and weirdly fibrillating chest. "Uh-oh," he said. "Whatta we got?"

Heshy didn't push me away — Heshy never could. Neither, frankly, did he hug me back. The sprightliest, most popular section of the Brandenburg Concertos emerged from the speaker next to which Heshy and I stood enmeshed — both of us, I now saw, miserably. The festive music slipped into the air around us like the voice of a lost love. We were in some kind of aftermath, and on the music all my loneliness flooded back in. As can happen in a dalliance with any loved and unavailable man, far from alleviating the misery of the life I had made outside this periodontal sanctuary, my moment with Heshy had only sharpened it.

I had to fix things! I let Heshy drop from my grip and the blood rushed back into his face.

At this point Dennis came through the office door.

"How did you get here?" I cried.

"Oh, hi there, Dennis!" This was Heshy, in the enervated tone of a hostage greeting the SWAT team.

Ignoring me, Dennis plunged into the hallway, and he and Heshy muttered and clapped each other's shoulders — some pathetic arcane masculine ritual that bought me time, before Den's hand clamped about my wrist and we sashayed from the office together as if willingly.

As we made our way out into caressing spring air, a carillon down the block seemed to be playing "Come Thou Almighty King." I would've wanted, of course, had I thought about it, to exit Heshy's into sunny silence, to stroll in sober contemplation, exactingly planning the methods I'd use to right everything that had gone so wildly awry. And now, alternatively, I was muddled and struggling and Dennis was attached to my arm. I was trying to keep alive what had been generated back there with Heshy and Sharon and the receptionist so long ago, that intense sense of belongingness, which feeling in any case was already being done an injury by the church bells, since I am not a Christian. Meanwhile Den was yanking me down the sidewalk, and I was setting my feet and having to be tugged along, like a totally pessimistic elderly woman being coaxed by her son-in-law into some umbrella-rimmed ocean.

Our Alfa was throbbing at the curb, its hazard lights blinking. We struggled toward it and Dennis pushed me in. And then Den was behind the wheel and I was drifting downward, down and down, dangling under my gentle marijuana parachute as we wound our serpentine path through oddly glittering Brooklyn en route to — where? He's taking me someplace strange! I snapped open my eyes. Sliding past was a house whose roof appeared to be holding up its columns rather than the reverse: the columns depended from the roof. This house scared me. Evidently I was still wrecked.

"So one doesn't," I said to Den after a long pulsating time, "have the normal reassurance of seeing a roof supported by its columns."

And he said, "What the hell is this now?" and then, "Normal? Normal? Is 'normal' an area with which you are familiar?" and looked at me blindly, and two cars honked and swerved. A Grand Cherokee pulled onto the sidewalk and the driver made as if to jump out and beat up my husband, but we zipped down the block. I smiled pleasantly and patted hubby's hand.

"I am not holding hands with you right now," he said. "You're telling me about 'normal' feelings?" Well, what-

ever my feelings — and I had many, and they were entwined and roiling — I didn't dignify that insulting
remark with a response. Frankly, I rehearsed telling him,
I don't know what in the world you are even talking
about.

Protruding from the backseat, Raleigh's head lay
between us, his pulse beating in his scalp. My gums
stung. I stretched my hand behind me to touch Raleigh's
back, to feel its heat, furriness, animal rise and fall.

With absolutely no stimuli at all, as I now cheerfully
said to myself, Dennis was growing enraged. He drove
with an impressive lunatic fervor, jerking the wheel and
accelerating randomly. Snot began to twitch at the edge
of his nostril. I cast him sidelong glances, entranced by
the life of this single bead of phlegm, its rhythmic appearance, disappearance, appearance. Inside his sweaty
shirt, his chest trembled.

After a long interesting mute time in our rocketing car,
he said grimly, "We are going to talk."

"Okey-dokey," I chirped.

But we didn't talk. I followed his lead; he followed mine.
Thus he continued to drive ferociously around Brooklyn pantomiming "a man at the end of his rope," while I
continued to observe "his high jinks" with a feeling both
malicious and serene. We rode in a busy silence. What a
long walk down a short hall. I was intermittently enjoying flashbacks to the perio office — mauvey color and a
feeling of being loved — and then finding myself back in

the car passing endless bodegas and restaurants, joggers and bikers, dogs that caused Raleigh to rear back and freak out, leafy parks, cozy private homes. My husband a hot, moist and oozing presence. From the backseat wafted doggy aromas, as Raleigh panted near my ear and slavered dog oil on my shoulder. We rode like spies, avoiding stops, reversing direction and zigzagging this way and that, as though we had some crucial secret to protect and perhaps, in appropriate secure conditions, should they ever arrive, to impart.

At last Dennis parked near a pier. "Get out," he said like a kidnapper, but it was only to walk Raleigh. The area was deserted except for, down the block, a single forlorn bar, undoubtedly harboring a demoralized day-time patron or two. Too bad we couldn't go in and chat them up. The pier was blocked off by a metal gate, and beyond it you could see the river and Manhattan. We started walking in circles, Den yanking on padlocks and pieces of chain-link fence, looking for a path to the water, and Raleigh hauling us this way and that.

Down the empty block, a short pale-brownish woman was walking our way, wearing, I now saw, the regalia of the Guardian Angels, the beloved citizens' patrol whose mission is to help make New York City safer. She stopped at the Alfa and walked around it, looking in the windows. "Hey!" Den yelled, and then he saw the red beret and jogged over to talk with her. It was cool out here and bright. Prickles of light glinted on the river. I could hear Dennis's voice tumbling over itself asking questions, but not the Guardian Angel's answers. Raleigh strained at the leash, nosing along the curb, and I watched the light falling down all around us. I was still a little high. Den started wildly waving me over.

"We're discussing the crime situation in the city here," he told me — excited and pleased, not at all as if he had recently dragged his wife from a dentist's office for a life-transforming chat. The Guardian Angel was short and solid, with a pretty, pointy face. She looked extremely tense.

Den: "This young woman offers a perfect sartorial representation of the role she has chosen — in effect, the *performance* she's going to do (Goffman has terrific stuff on this, the congruence between appearance and manner in the context of performance). (This is my wife.) See, honey? The beret of a paratrooper, but it's scarlet, the color of passion."

Me: "And of blood. Hi."

The Guardian Angel: "How ya doin'."

Den: "Camouflage pants. Black cat-burglar-type gloves. No weapon, of course. You know the Guardian Angels don't carry weapons, don't you?"

Me: "Yes."

Den: "Goffman would've loved this; it's just got so much complex meaning. The fierce stance, the peaceful intentions — no gun, correct? Guardian Angels don't carry guns, right?"

The Guardian Angel: "They never do."

Den, importantly: "You do martial arts, I think."

The Angel: "Me personally, myself, no — I don't have free time."

Den: "But I know you guys used to have what's called a *shaolin* temple someplace in the Bronx — you still have that?"

The Angel: "Yeah, they don't have that now."

Den: "Medals on the hat like a military person, but on close inspection they're just pins and decorative little doodads."

The Guardian Angel: "Shit, man, these are not doo-dads."

Den, still energetically climbing toward a peak of soci-ology: "What *front* you guys present! Handcuffs clipped onto the garrison belt, but how often do you ever use them? Only to make a citizen's arrest, right? And the whole outfit just brilliantly conveys the Guardian Angels' values and goals — we see military precision, strength, vigilance, but also order, compassion —"

Me: "Compassion?"

The Guardian Angel: "These handcuffs, man?" She unclipped them from her belt. Raleigh jumped in place, thinking she was going to throw a ball. Den stepped toward the woman, she toward him, and Raleigh thrashed, and she slipped the cuffs on Den's wrists and clicked them shut.

Dennis grinned uncertainly.

The Guardian Angel turned her back to the street and slid a big pistol out of her jacket and pointed it at me. She said to Den: "You move or you yell, man, and I shoot this girlfriend."

Den (whispering, flapping his handcuffed hands): "What! You're not a Guardian Angel!"

The Angel moved in close, pressed the barrel into Den's belly, and whispered back: "No talking or I shoot your dog also."

At the mention of killing Raleigh, I wet my pants. Raleigh, still alive, pressed his snuffling nose against my slub silk trousers and frantically sniffed. Den, almost inaudibly: "I'll talk if I want to."

Me: "Should I get his wallet for you? He can't reach his wallet."

The Angel: "Yeah, you do it now."

Den (tears in his voice): "I can't even resist because you might kill somebody I love."

The Angel, reasonably: "And you give me everything. You keep back something, I kill you anyway."

Den: "You fake."

Me: "Dennis. Shut up."

Den: "Uh! Uh! Uh! Uh!" Samsonlike, he was struggling against his cuffs.

The Angel: "This guy is like — you can't know what he's gonna do, right?"

Me: "Yes. He's unpredictable."

The Angel: "That's very difficult."

Den: "Don't even converse with her, honey. She's a total phony."

The Angel: "I had a guy like this. *Very messy too,* right? Stuff all over the house all the time? It got so bad I was thinking maybe I just kill him. You know how they say? Just 'take him out of his misery.' I know you have that thought. Oh, I'm sorry! You pee your pants."

Me: "That's okay."

The Angel: "I'm sorry, though. Oh, I like those ear-rings, like little fishes. I could take them, but I can't wear them." She leaned in to show me her right ear, where the lobe had been ripped by an earring's being yanked straight down. "This is something the guy did acciden-tally — I'm not telling you how; you wouldn't believe this one."

Den: "You bogus person. You complete nonentity. She's not a Guardian Angel."

The Angel: "I would like to be one, but I need to make money. Inside your wallet maybe I got enough to fly to L.A. Get in your car. You keep those handcuffs, man. Look nice on you! I'm using my other pair on your wife." We got in. She shoved Raleigh down into a sitting position and he licked her hand. And to me: "I don't know. Good luck."

Then she cuffed me to the Alfa's leather-covered steering wheel and ran behind a warehouse and she was gone. Raleigh watched after her as though he'd been jilted at the altar.

I started to tremble and couldn't stop. I honked the horn and shrieked myself hoarse for forty-five minutes before a patrol car pulled up and two cops, blasé to the point of near-total muteness, opened the doors and released us, and in all that time Dennis said not a word. He was disconsolate, I would find out weeks later, t primarily because he had misread the "front" and urately anticipated the "performance" and not n that she would "break frame," but because he mugged by a girl. At the precinct house, when they asked us what had happened, I cried and Dennis blushed.

In the aftermath of the mugging, Den and I reached a pitch, together, of contentless hostility. The next morning, deep in my marijuana hangover, I backed the Alfa into the street, whereupon Dennis promptly came around the corner in my van and rear-ended me. My neck snapped. In a fury I leaped from the car, landing so hard my soles stung. I pointed and screamed like a person in a silent movie: "You!"

To our surprise, he yelped back, and then we yelled together a remarkably long time, not, unfortunately, with the pure refreshing vengefulness of insulted strangers, but, instead, with the confused agenda of people who think they know each other only too well. Young Wesley Rolfe was on his stoop today, with his head completely under his T-shirt, tactfully ignoring me and Dennis along with the rest of the borough of Brooklyn. As a bored crowd gathered, I called my husband's problems "pathology" and he called me "sick."

Suddenly I broke off. I leaped at Den and handed him the keys. Then I left the Alfa in the street with its door open and Dennis swimming through a sea of honks and sarcastic advice. I went up the steps, into my own house, his and mine, and I stood in the kitchen looking into the refrigerator for a long time. We had learned that when the refrigerator was too full Den got overstimulated, so it was stocked, preventively, as lightly as possible: kosher spears, twelve red grapes softening in their plastic webbing, an empty six-pack carton, and some flavored waters. Sad supplies. Far away, Den's voice, small, continued to contend with passersby, while cold air settled around me and my pulse slowed.

Well, you can't cure loneliness any of the ways I tried.

13

The day Dennis smashed my toe was the day he first avoided my eyes. I almost feel the guy never looked at me again.

Travel Light magazine wanted me to take pictures in Hana, apparently a barely accessible town on Maui, traditionally inhabited by cows, rock stars who drop from the sky in private planes, and ordinary Hawaiians with pickups; then the crater at sunrise. Of course I said I'd do it. For the first time since Dennis and I had started whatever it was we had started, I would be leaving town.

Plotting like a prisoner, careful not to arouse suspicion, folding clothes with gingerly attention to detail, I packed. Two days from now, I'd be flown.

That night Dennis (scrubbed and gleaming — you could never predict) stroked at my hair and tirelessly rubbed my back, lying near me like an unusual but true courtesan, penis semi-erect, soap in his ears. He talked to me for hours. How glad he was to see me have this nice opportunity, how sorry to see me go away even temporarily, how much he loved me, although he knew he sometimes appeared distracted — *was* distracted! *was!* — but this distraction wasn't about anything to do with me, or us, or our marriage, or the home we'd made together here so artfully in the short time we'd tried; how our bond was the strongest thing in his life; that if he were somehow to lose me, the loss would be irreparable; that without me he'd . . .

There was no moon. No light streamed in. We lay in blackness, staring up. Now he was holding my hand — not too tightly, but while he talked he was squeezing it rhythmically with a delicate, tender, weird pulsing, more unnerving than his usual crushing hold.

He said he'd learned something this year: that if he lost me he'd be lost himself; we could not be parted — temporarily, yes, but permanently, no — regardless of evelopments; if I were considering leaving him, I uld know something, and he wanted to say it clearly, o annoy me, not to menace me, certainly not to dare *rtainly not to frighten me,* not to judge and not to but he wanted to articulate an idea — a fact, it — with which, he had recently discovered, we after always live.

vas this: I could not leave him.

go, he had to say, but this was not intended t was the furthest thing from his mind,

'm going for one week."

Outside, as if in deep snow, Brooklyn had fallen still. The darkness in here was so thick and soft.

Extremely unusual squeezing. Pulse. Pulse. He apologized but he needed to finish his comments. He needed to tell me what he had learned, about men, and women, and life, and connection, and truly, above all, about marriage — about what his life with me had taught him.

It was this:

If I tried to leave him, he would not let me do it.

The next morning we woke pallid and clogged up from excessive all-night conversation.

I shuffled into the kitchen, where, early as it was, he was already trying to prepare a frittata in a cast-iron pan. He was pouring eggs with trembling hands. "I'm cooking for you! Leave the room! You can make the coffee but then you leave."

I was gray and puffy. The floor was cool under my bare feet, and my nightdress itched. Got the grounds out of the freezer, found a paper filter, set it in the cone, opened a drawer for a spoon, backed toward Den but didn't touch him. He felt me there and twitched and, shaking off the twitch, stumbled, and he lurched against the stove, and the loop of his khakis caught on the skillet's handle while he turned, and his pants yanked the skillet, and the eggs slid inside it, and the skillet fell, we saw it falling. It landed on my left foot.

Even now that big toe is too wide, flattened like a cartoon thumb that's been whacked by a cartoon hammer.

In the moment, as in that same depressing vignette, a starburst of pain. I screamed and the scene glimmered and fractured. What I saw — confetti of green pepper, curds of egg, clock, pot holders, terracotta floor shifting, Raleigh's tail flapping, shelf of cookbooks and Cuisinart and sunlight and plates, and Den, aghast — everything shattered into fragments that rained into my eyes. Pain jumped out of place and went somewhere, and I went with it. Nausea flooding. Clatter. Sparkle gone and blackness dropping down. I fell onto big glazed rust-colored tiles, felt coolness, and then the black folded over me and I slept.

I couldn't go to Maui — waking on the floor, I knew this. I woke up floating in the disaffected and passive wife's ordinary dream, planning for him to book a ticket himself, board, buckle in and take off, and his plane to crash.

Saturday, ninety degrees, and the streets were quiet — one million rich people had gone to the beach. This time the emergency room doc was a steely, absurdly overworked young woman who looked at Dennis hard. (Den: "What's your point? I didn't do it on purpose.") She closed us into separate rooms and walked pessimistically between us, hearing his story and checking it against mine. "I'm getting a feeling of possible problems at home," she told me, and I shocked us both by spilling out a big reedy inappropriate laugh, before denying everything. At last the doc, with a pointed air of "it's your funeral," shot me with tetanus toxoid and taped a splint on my toe. He had cracked it in seventeen places.

Then I was in bed, in blasts of air-conditioner wind, under two blankets, drifting on Percocet and sinking.

It was late when I woke. The air conditioner was still, the window open, and the heat had blown away. I could see rooftops and a bright night sky. Raleigh was sighing somewhere in the dark. Dennis wasn't in the bed, though I could feel him in the house. Far across Brooklyn, a siren. And, somewhere nearer, weeping.

It took a long time, using one crutch and jumping on my right foot, to locate him. He was locked in the bathroom.

Den! Den!

As in every story about a troubled marriage that we have ever heard, he wouldn't let me in.

As you'd expect, I yelled, *"Open the door."* Naturally he refused: "I'm not opening the fucking door!" He was snuffling, and I was balanced on one foot. Near dawn. The "fucking door" between us. As everybody knows, with tedious predictability I had to murmur near the fucking door's edge and plead and remind him of my injury and that it was too difficult for me to hop back to bed without assistance and that I loved him and that he should *not continue to* —

He turned the lock.

Inside, light was blazing. Because of an earlier plumbing mishap (which I prefer not to go into), the walls were Sheetrocked instead of plastered, and now Den, late at night, alone, realizing he had broken his wife's toe, had locked himself in, started to cry recklessly, and kicked the shit out of his favorite bathroom. Beside the mirror was a hole in the wall, two panes had been punched out of the window, the shower curtain was heaped on the floor and Dennis was stamping around on it, sniffing. His face was pink and streaming. I wished intensely that I'd brought a camera. I was behind my painkiller. Even so, it occurred to me to spring at his throat.

Dennis looked away. Leaning on the door, protecting my toe, I watched him winking, sniffling, and attempting to wrap a yellow hand towel around his bloody meaty hand. After a while I said the only thing I could think of: "This is just one more mess."

At the word "mess," my husband began to weep as expressively, wetly, and loudly as I've ever heard a man do. "I'm a *boor*," he cried. "I'm a *fool*. I love you so much, *so much*, I love you more than anything, and I'm really trying, and *I try all the time,* and all I ever do is *fuck it up. I fuck it up! I fuck it up! I fuck it up!*" He sobbed, banged at himself, and shook his head like a dog so that tears flipped all around the room. Back in the bedroom, Raleigh woke up. He barreled down the hall, pushed past me, and, with lovely mute canine loyalty, stood next to Dennis.

"Honey," I said. I hopped from the door to the sink.

"Don't come in here," he sobbed. *"It's dangerous in here with me in here."*

I leaned against the sink, reached for his wrapped hand and tugged at the towel, and he pulled away. "I can't chase you," I said.

Over his shoulder: *"Keep away from me! You'll get your fucking legs broken!"*

But finally, tears plopping off his nose, self-hating Dennis let me untie his bloody towel. I held the cut hand under hot water and soaped it for a long time. He grew quiet — not peaceful, but docile. My anger was gone, and in its place was a smoother, darker feeling, something I thought I might look at later, something almost like despair. After I washed the guy's hand there was mud in the sink.

This is what I dreamed in my Percocet haze:

He crawls down the stairs on his belly, carpet sliding under him, lint in his nose, his face slick with tears. Then he's upright at night in the garden, among dogwoods, young Wes Rolfe's flying clubs, and white blossoms shining in the dark. A shadow moves. Somebody stabs him! Then we hold his funeral on a sunny day.

My latest injury seemed to further transform Dennis, making him obliquely vigilant, nervous about letting me out of his sight, and, what was most dramatic, subdued. Desultorily, he bought me bunches of gifts, just anything in the stores nearest our house — small appliances, undergarments, cheese. He'd carry them home and present them hopelessly, sidling up like Raleigh when he'd been a bad dog. "Oh thank you," I'd cry, with a high-wattage grin. He was so sweet, and I felt daily guiltier. "It's not great but at least I got something," he'd mutter. Or worse: "Don't thank me."

Much of my time now was consumed in bathing and preparing to bathe — I couldn't get my broken toe wet in the shower, so I'd inch up to the third floor to lie in the tub with my foot propped on the edge. Dennis wanted to come to my aid — hold my elbow, carry the towels — but I wouldn't let him. Den said he planned, one of these days, to join me while I enjoyed a good soak, to hunker down in the wicker chair and read me some of his writings, and, hearing that friendly idea, I was afraid with a chihuahua's fear. I started keeping space between us so he couldn't trample me or something — I would just widen the gap when he wasn't exactly looking, which was always.

Ambulatory life forgotten. Nights, I held my left foot, with its slowly regenerating toe, off the bed out of harm's way; this activity kept me up until morning. When I lay near him, I felt so sympathetic. When I slept, I slept watchfully, up near the surface like a bird in my nest of fears, one eye open against my dangerous husband.

And I started to dream — not yet to think — of the drastic steps I'd be taking to save my life.

I had been in this house for long silent unrecoverable days. I had to get out. *Travel Light* said they'd send me in a car to the South Street Seaport — shots of dazed tourists and barges on the river. I limped out and did it.

At four o'clock, as I returned from this first outing, when I rounded our corner a delivery van was trying to park sideways, and Dennis was in the street, yelling, running around, and holding back traffic with his palm. Emerging from the van was a Victorian porcelain clawfoot bathtub, the world's widest and deepest. Here's what it was: Den's gift to me.

Five guys nudged the tub down the ramp, hefted it up the front steps, and stood in the foyer holding it, their faces reddening and sweat starting to drop into their eyes, while, too slowly, Den understood that to maneuver the tub around the landing we'd have to remove the banisters. The guys backed out, set the tub on the sidewalk, climbed up the steps again patient as saints, and spent an hour surgically separating the banisters from the stairs. Then they went back and hoisted up the tub and, conferring monosyllabically, tried to shove it upstairs.

They staggered like pallbearers, mourners for a giant. "Won't go, man." But he pleaded, so they tried. At the curve at the head of the stairs, they rested a clawed foot in the coffin niche, but still they couldn't swing it. All the while, Den getting his feet under theirs, wedging himself between them and the wall, and filling the air with offers of assistance and heartfelt thanks. *Thanks, guys. Thanks a lot, guys.*

Won't go, they said.

Still he insisted. It meant so much to him that they tried again. At the curve at the top of the stairs, the five bearers bulged and lurched in place. Still it wouldn't go.

Again they backed out. They answered every question and they waited until he got out of the way. They gave him the time he needed and they had all the time in the world. I would say that the immense and spontaneous graciousness of these five strangers was an inspiration to me, if the model they offered hadn't been so obviously completely out of range. In fact in many lifetimes, I already knew, I would never be able to begin to follow the example of these stalwart, tolerant, empathic men. They shamed me. I couldn't behave as they did on my most forbearing day during my maturest week. And they were doing it while carrying a bathtub.

(In the end, I should mention, it became apparent that the tub couldn't be carried upstairs and would have to be lifted up the side of the building by a crane. No problem. For a man of real generosity and resourcefulness, no problem. Den got a crane. Two carpenters went upstairs and removed two windows and a section of wall. This was quite instructive: It turned out to be easier for a Komatsu crane to put a bathtub into the third story of a brownstone than for my husband, Dennis, to amble downstairs without mishap any random morning. But how was that Dennis's fault? But you can't rush up and whisper to an unknown crane driver, *Take me away*.)

He insisted I use it, and, truthfully, I did want to. It was a gorgeous tub, milky, chalky, silvery, blank. But so large that now he had to help me in and out — every day he boosted me over the side. I'd sink in warm water, the plashing would quiet, the mirror would fog over, and he'd still be standing there, looking the other way.

"I'm fine," I'd say finally.

At last, trampling the rag rug, he'd leave.

Escape. Escape. I'd suppress the thought, crush it hard. But the idea was starting to lie there anyway, one of those bugs too flat to squash.

Alone in the room, low in the pearly bath, my injured foot resting on the sweep of edge, I started to remember Bianca. Though Dennis visited her twice daily, I hadn't shaken flakes into her bucket in weeks. Here I was, away from the sun, alabaster reflecting off the walls of my porcelain container, and I was blanching, lying in my summer coffin turning slowly, truly white. The dead marmoreal color of — what? Of guilt for my unkind thoughts. Of aloneness. Of fear. I felt a kinship with an albino frog! Some etiolated thing under a lid, like a plant trying to grow in darkness! I was depressed! Bianca at the bottom of the house, me at the top; rushing between us a madman, but *our* man.

That afternoon, the day I recalled her, I struggled into the basement for the first time in a while. It took ten minutes to get down the stairs, descending into coolness and dark. I leaned my crutch on Den's tool shelf, spread newspapers on the cement floor, and sat. I opened the lid. There she was, hanging in her bucket pond. "Hi," I said.

Hi, Bianca would've said, in some other, more magical story. Long time no see.

"I'm in trouble," I said.

Exactly, she would've said. And you've made your own trouble. You continue to make and remake it. By the way, did you close the door so the dog can't get me?

Her voice would be piping — not like the peep of the one-inch-long spring peeper, which carries a mile, and no bullfrog's foghorn, no toad ventriloquism, but a lovely sound, direct and mellow and sweet. I looked in. She hung perfectly still, opalescent in the dusk of the cellar. I asked, "What should I do?"

Never forget my need for copper. Keep putting the pennies in the water.

"I mean for myself."

Anybody you could talk to?

"That's part of it. I had friends — but they're gone, somehow."

How?

"Some moved away. Some I don't really hear from anymore. Most of them we . . . lost. Anyway, I'd ask a friend what I'm asking you. What should I do?"

We waited for Bianca to consider. She hung there as if she had expired recently at some frog peak of health and plumpness.

I said, "I can't go places easily — it's hard to get around. Just walking out to take a few pictures is hard."

So maybe you need to stay home awhile.

"I'm freaking out here."

So maybe you need to get out of here, whatever it takes.

"I do have to. I gotta get out! Should I try somehow to get away for even a week? I could maybe think things over."

My Bianca: Can you drive?

"My van's automatic, not stick."

So no clutch.

"Right."

So Dennis could stay with me, and you could be alone and listen to your breath or whatever. And get a take on the complicated screwup you're involved in here.

"Danger. It's like a kind of — well, *that:* danger."

Whatever. Anyway, complicated.

"Does that sound plausible to you?" In the grotto of the cellar, my voice echoed coolly. It broke my heart, hearing my own hungry question. I was sitting on the business section on a floor in a basement in Brooklyn, among fuse boxes and water pipes, favoring a broken toe and gazing into a bucket. "Should I go away?"

If she could have, the frog definitely would've answered, Go.

14

A moment came when I looked around and almost nobody was there. The truth is, I had lost track of even my devoted friend Sallie. She and I had — what? Drifted apart.

Frankly, there were others we had managed to lose: not only Sallie; our housekeeper, Luz; Den's squash partner, Pudney; and Lydia, who'd sort of introduced us even though (or perhaps *because,* as I now began to suspect) we hadn't really known her. But also our high school friends, our college friends, our former lovers, and the rest of the guests at our wedding. Before they disappeared I had photographed many of them, and somewhere along the line we had lost the prints.

Our remaining friends were: Donald the percussionist, who had watched us marry and seen us begin our shared life and promptly moved to Providence to play *cumbia* and *gaita* with some Colombians. (He had immediately sent two Paw Sox caps — then nothing. Still, I consider him, indefensibly perhaps, to have belonged, at the time we're considering, on the active list.)

And my girlhood friend Jane, who lived in Kentucky and whom I hadn't spoken to in two years.

And Wesley Rolfe, the next-door juggler. I include him because I had the strong presentiment that he and I would soon communicate more directly with each other — we might speak; we might share a moment.

And Tommy, the wine store owner, and the guy in the bagel place across the street: people we paid to know us. No, that's a bad comment, bitter, unfunny, and untrue. I should affirm that both Tommy and the bagel guy actually enjoyed Dennis for himself. It was sweet. They loved to see him grinning and waving and cranking up to wrestle the door open; they loved to hear his warble as, inevitably, he tripped on the sill. Those undiscriminating jerks didn't have to live in this house.

Helping me out of the bathtub, he dropped me. As I hit the tile floor, it occurred to me to play dead.

Two days later I clumped back down. Raleigh tailed me, nose in my butt, but I shoved him back up and slammed the door. Under the lid, there she hung.

Reproach was in the basement air — she was lonely too. "I've been upstairs," I said.

I assumed, she would've said.

"I didn't say anything to him."

She hung there: So you're not going away.

"I guess not right now. I can't seem to bring it up."

Maybe now is not the time.

"Maybe I just have to stay home awhile and try to fig-ure things out here."

So you'll be around.

"I guess so."

So what's wrong?

"I'm afraid. I'm stuck. I'm screwing up, and I can't break out."

That's true.

"I think Dennis and I might be more entwined than I knew."

Bianca: You certainly are.

"I need some friends."

This we mentioned.

"I think maybe the most important thing I could do right now, while my toe is healing, is to find some friends."

The white frog would've said: If you're down in a cellar discussing your life with me, that pretty much proves your point. How about dechlorinating my water and shaking some brine-shrimp flakes into it near my mouth?

I'm talking to an amphibian. I need human beings.

But it seemed I didn't, anymore, know how you found them. I phoned my old friend Jane in Kentucky; she didn't recognize my voice. But then she was delighted to hear from me after all this long time, listened for an hour, and said my story, lengthy, convoluted and fundamentally inexplicable as it was, just tugged her heart. "You can handle it, honey," she said, because *she* would've been able to. Her children had gone away, to Haverford and Harvard. All day she made erotic drawings, smudging the charcoal with her fingers, reaching sundown spent and happy with her hands all black. She had a new lover, a smart, big-shouldered, top-heavy man from New Orleans, a personal friend of the Neville brothers. Late, he would walk in moonlight across the yards from his house to hers and climb the stairs like an angel; he would do that longed-for thing: come to her in the night. I could feel it so well, shadows of lush low-growing trees, the white moon gleaming, the creak of Aaron Neville's step on the stair, his mouth on her skin. Oh I was lost. She asked, "Can't anybody help you?" But there was nobody.

"Or *can't you leave* that damn husband?"

Of course. I had to. "No," I said.

Instead, I took us to a party.

Sometimes, as we know, things can suddenly seem almost manageable, even hopeful, when you just step out and leave your own home behind. I trimmed my crutch with streamers. Didn't bring a camera.

It was our new neighbors' Sunday-afternoon housewarming. We didn't know these neighbors and they didn't know us — I have to assume that's why we got the invite. The house was grand, with a river view. It had just been redecorated in every corner and was filled with the palest colors — rosy glass lampshades, celadon ceilings, sea green tiles surrounding the fireplace, satiny paint like cream brushed onto the walls. The hosts, a rich young couple, were beautiful. As I say, we didn't know them, and we never would. She wore one silver earring like a strand of tears falling alongside her neck. The teardrops jerked as Den took her hand, backed up, and knocked over the hall table.

"Oh gosh. I'm sorry!"

"No no, it's fine, it's —"

"I'll just —"

"No no, don't worry. We'll —"

I think I will never forget how promptly I turned my back on the man I had just introduced as my husband and clumped toward the din of the party. For that incomparable moment, quitting the foyer, I knew myself to be, however blameworthy, confident and vindictive and desperate: My toe may be smashed but I can still step out of the debris.

And then I was in the next room and I was searching for what I needed. Standing near the bass player was a young woman, quiet in the animated crowd, pierced of course and wearing the customary brutal ensemble — black scraps and powerful boots. She stood under a cloud of bluish black hair, listening to the music with an amiable daughterly look. She could become my nice young groover pal. I leaned on my crutch and started lurching forward. But then a young man leaped across the rug, reached her, and dived under her hair. I stopped. She already had a person.

At the bar, I talked with another woman. She had a grin made of completely regular small teeth. She wore red. We leaned our heads together and conferred with that instantaneous, deft, confiding frankness of dynamic women just meeting in a debased world full of problematic romantic partners all problematic in roughly identical ways (I was rusty, but this skill comes back fast). I so badly wanted this woman to become my friend that when I found out she was moving to Palo Alto, I staggered into the dove gray powder room and wept into the little brushed-steel sink.

Somewhere, when I returned, I could hear Dennis chortling; I moved away until the sound faded. I looked for young Wesley Rolfe, but of course he hadn't been invited. I would not flag. I would find somebody.

I met, at the fruit-salad bowl, a man as artfully tinted as the house — brown gold skin, pink gold hair, champagne-colored eyelashes. He was tanned so evenly he looked as though he'd been turned on a spit. At the risk of sounding offensively reifying, I can tell you he was a perfect piece of toast. The air here smelled of melons, and in that scent the man and I chatted. With a toothpick he was working his way through some honeydew balls. I held up my wounded foot, and he looked at it. Then a woman sneaked up and leaned against one side of him, and the man set his hand on the nape of her neck and rested it there, gold down flashing. Then he chewed more melon while this woman and I thought together about his hot hand. All that night in Den's and my bed, I already knew, I would see his orotone glow instead of darkness behind my eyes.

Again I could hear Dennis, from another room. I didn't look.

In the corner, a bunch of sweaty gray people were muttering together, stumbling in place as if they'd been on call for thirty-six hours. They looked different from the other guests — no Boss jackets, no rubber jewelry, and they were wrecks. I had met a couple of them before: They were writers. One was a guy whose jacket photo I had taken for his third volume of poems. (For the shoot he had worn an unpressed white dress shirt and jeans and stood in his Carroll Street garden in dappled light for three hours, twitching with nerves every time the shutter blinked. This was odd for a poet — they were ordinarily steely as hit men. Finally I took him to the park and shot him in shade under a locust tree. On the back of his book he appears, beneath the leaves, soulful to the point of being suicidal.)

The other writers were shifting their weight and pretending to listen with their gray faces as the poet told them a joke. After squeezing a couple of wan chuckles out of his audience, the poet decamped for the bar. I was left loitering there — because of my toe, I couldn't quickly move away. The nearest person was a tall young man who looked like a grade school boy; he seemed as discouraged in this festive room in this moment of levity as the poet had been in pitiless black and white. I said, "I didn't get the punch line."

"You missed a big moment."

"What was it?"

"Not worth hearing."

"Tell me anyway."

Glumly, he held up two fingers. " 'You're two tents.' "

"I don't get it."

"Forget it."

"What does it mean?"

"Will you forget the joke? It's a really stupid joke."

"But is it —?"

"Are you one of these incredibly persistent anxiety-ridden women who's fundamentally deaf to everything she hears but like a dog with a bone no matter what it is?"

Gee, maybe yes. Then we introduced ourselves.

"You're a writer, right?"

"And other things."

"What other things?"

"Let me tell you when I know you better."

"You can't tell me now?"

"I can. But I'm not going to."

"Can you give me a hint?"

"No."

"It's something illegal, isn't it?"

"You're a woman with only one move, huh?"

"I'm just asking."

He grinned darkly and looked away.

"I can almost tell, the way you're looking, that it's some kind of illegal —"

"Hey. Look at me. Not now. You appear likeable, but you're gonna have to stop badgering me or I'm walking away. Is this something you can comprehend? I'm not gonna tell you when you're ready. I'm gonna tell you when *I'm* ready."

So, in the last possible instant, I had made a friend.

15

After his hand healed from punching the bathroom wall, Den got a complicated cold. He stopped washing his hair daily, and sometimes he slept on his hair so that he spent the following day with the demented look of a stuffed chick that's been mashed in a kid's Easter basket.

Now Dennis, about whom some decision increasingly begged to be made, started to almost smell, a bit. His jackets started, I suppose, to hold old sweat. I took the jackets to the cleaners, and they came back pressed, their sleeves stuffed with paper, the scent still there. He stopped hanging the jackets and started keeping them on chairs, rolled into lumps.

In those days, Dennis still showered — I heard the shower running every morning as I woke — but it was as though he didn't. I say I know he showered. One morning I rose early to be sure. Limped quietly to stand outside the bathroom in the hall, on the runner, that familiar flowered carpet — cabbage roses with pointed leaves, petals of maroon and cream — upon which I'd stood forever ago, more than a year ago, gazing out into friendly Brooklyn and wondering what was to come. Now I loitered in that place listening to rain in the bathroom and recognizing what it was I actually, creepily, believed: that Dennis was in there running the shower but standing outside the stall.

I turned the knob and went in. Raleigh, recumbent on chenille, held still but opened and shifted his eyes. His tail thumped. "Don't worry, I'm not going to kick you out," I told him.

"What? What?" Den yelled. On the shower curtain, seashells — violet snails and moon snails, cowries and conchs — slid across aquamarine vinyl. Den was behind the curtain: He was in there!

I took a few shots of the shells; of Raleigh with his head between his paws; of the newly spackled hole in the wall; of the two newly glazed windowpanes; of the magnifying mirror, deodorant sticks, sweating tiles, cloudy air. I stood in the fragrant steam with a reason to be here, soothed every time the shutter clicked. Dennis didn't hear me. And later, when I showed him the prints, he didn't recognize the scene.

As it happens, now I was shooting several rolls daily. I shot his mashed hair. His averted eyes.

Once in a while — not often, but not only once — he had food on the fronts of his teeth! But mystery foods. Nothing I'd seen him eat, nothing from our fridge.

I shot: his smile.
I started calling him: he.

I had a gardenia on my table. I was keeping it moist. My gardenia was my pal.

Day 400: Dennis, wet — a photographic record of his having showered.

Day 412: Dennis and me fully dressed. Me lurking far behind him, my toe still bandaged. Den's shirt unimaginably crumpled; his right hand bandaged. His fingers apparently quite clean.

Day 413: Dennis and me, dressed and bandaged. Den looking away from me. Den grinning, flashing ruddy gums.

Day 414: Dennis, sleeve rolled, and a big Band-Aid, black around the edges, protecting a mystery gash on his forearm. Me, cheek bruised where he accidentally clobbered me with his elbow. Still bandaged (today freshly), the couple's toe and hand.

He got lice. He scratched wildly and ran from room to room; in two short days he covered his scalp with scabs.

My list of questions for the dermatologist: Can you put the shampoo on shoulders and neck and face? Can they live on the plastic earpieces of glasses? Do they carry other diseases? Will they definitely die inside a closed plastic bag? How long will they live in, say, a jacket, or upholstery, if not disturbed? Can you redo the shampoo over and over until you're convinced they're dead?

I drove Dennis to the doctor, demanded to go in with him. I read off my questions, adding an inspired impromptu last-minute one: Should I throw out his jackets? "Settle down," the dermatologist said. "Lice are not fleas." He added that lice didn't usually come from dirtiness but simply from exposure, and Dennis glared at me and I cut him dead. "I got them in the movies," Den told us, and we stared at him.

Dennis and I joined each other in the bathroom to wash his hair with nit-killing shampoo; he couldn't do it alone — he'd blind himself.

That night Dennis wept. I heard him, very late. I hadn't spoken to him since the lice diagnosis, but his snuffles woke me and weakened my resolve. "What is it?"

"Nothing," he said. Then: "Discouragement."

"You're sad?"

"I think so," he said. "It doesn't interest me, though."

Flies entered our life together. They hatched and flew. We rolled a couple of dish towels and chased them, swatting at the windowsills as they sat rubbing their legs together, and into the air as they buzzed and rushed the lightbulbs. We left their corpses where they fell. Hairy black gumdrops crushed in the kitchen.

My toenail turned black and fell off. He saw it. He seemed about to cry, which I ignored. Forget it, Dennis, I thought. No more black-and-white shots of our lachrymose hero, I thought, with his wet eyes shining.

Around the house, I limped, he slunk. We spoke little and then graciously. With our reticence and politeness, we signaled our wish to imagine, while we bought time, something like peace.

The life of the brownstone became animated, full of color and sound, as though he and I were inside a true silence and the house were speaking for us.

The coffee machine's three plaintive beeps.

The metallic snap and fizz of his Diet Pepsi being popped open two rooms away.

The click of Raleigh's nails on polished floor.

Dennis had bought me a bathtub. He was a wonderful, beautiful soul. But love had drained from the noisy house.

One day he phoned while I was home alone, and when he said my name, I thought it was a crank call — I did not immediately recognize my husband's voice. I hung up.

He called back. "That was you," he said.

"What was me?" So it had been Dennis!

"Just now, when I called."

"When?" I asked.

"Why did you hang up?"

"When?"

"Why did you hang up just now, when I called?"

"I didn't," I said. "What are you talking about? Did you call here? It wasn't me."

"I just called. You know I called. You answered the phone and you hung up on me. Why did you do that?"

"I didn't. The phone didn't ring here until this call right now."

"I recognized you. It *was* you. It was *you*."

"No. It wasn't. The phone didn't ring."

"Stop it! I know it was you!"

"Dennis!" I cried. *"Why would I pretend I didn't know you?"*

He was breathing hard, as after a fast ascent. He sounded scared.

"Why would I *do* that?" I demanded. I really wanted to know.

Breathing.

"Why would I do something like that?"

After a long pause and, as you are aware, correctly: "What I know is that you did."

The next day a neighbor asked me what my husband's name was, and I couldn't recall. I pretended I hadn't heard; she asked again. I stalled — I started swatting at myself, portraying a woman being bitten by a bug. The letters of his name began slowly to appear in my head. At last I said, "It's Dennis," but without conviction.

That night I told him, "I forgot your name."

"Don't worry about it," he said, and he grinned and spilled all the coffee out of his mug. In concert we swabbed hopelessly, as so often before, at the soaked carpet.

Don't worry about it.

Don't worry about it.

This is what people say to each other. But what could they possibly mean?

16

My toe healed. I agreed to an assignment, a piece about Provincetown, color portraits of painters with their work. "I need to be away for a week, okay?" He guessed so, he said, and I allowed a barely plausible amount of time to pass, then kissed his cheek, ran to the Alfa, threw off the tarp, and peeled out.

I drove to Massachusetts without stopping, and out the Cape as it curved and narrowed, and checked in to a cottage in North Truro on the bay. I parked the car behind the cottage on a patch of crushed quahog shells, set down my bag, washed my face, drove into town, ate kale soup, and went to *Jurassic Park*. In the dark for hours, my heart thumped, and when the dinos swept like ladies in waiting through the glade, tears stood in my eyes. Peace. The lost world. I drove back to the cottage and sat on the bed in the dark. Across the bay, Provincetown glittered like the lights of a foreign city.

All week it rained. No Cape light. All week the Hassel-blad and the Nikon lay on the table wearing their lens caps — hibernating cameras, shuttered and sleeping. All week I drove into town and ate and walked and drove back, and sat in the damp cottage under an amazingly low fiberboard ceiling, looking through a patched screen at rain slanting into Cape Cod Bay, and tried to think and tried to plan. Couldn't.

I called the magazine and said it was raining so the piece wouldn't work and anyway the artists were not amenable and in fact I had been meaning to mention I was planning to embark on a sort of sabbatical for a while, and —

Fine, they said. Let's just kill it.

At night I dreamed and saw me and Dennis eyeing each other in a room like a box, its walls closing while we didn't notice we were about to be crushed. Had I been in the care of a psychoanalyst, this unerring fantasy would never have been mentioned, I can tell you. As the walls touched, I woke into a bright rainy dawn.

I sat on the bed and reviewed our assets.

Dennis had only his mother; and I had my friend Jane in Kentucky, my friend Sallie who had stopped calling, and two cousins near Cleveland. Den and I were each other's family.

We had Bianca. We had Raleigh.

And we had the cat, the small orange moiré-patterned cat named Icarus, formerly Ginger Girl, who lived in the front hall closet, whose bowls sat in the downstairs bathroom because she was terrified of the kitchen. She was so reclusive that I almost never thought of her; still, she was with us. Instead of ending in points, the cat's ears were rounded, giving her a cute mutant-pet look. When she was a kitten, while her mother was out, the tips of Ginger Girl's ears had been burned off in a grease fire started by Dennis (he had readily told me), who had got the broiler going and then left the room to locate his glasses. By the time he returned, the fire had eaten half the kitchen, where baby Ginger Girl was living her wobbly life in a pile of siblings in a box next to the oven, and Den had dropped a towel over his head and blasted through smoke and flames and rescued the four singed fluffballs. Only after they were saved did he dial 911. At no moment had he even fleetingly considered the potential cost of future renovation, or the safety of his entire big brownstone, or the brownstone next door, or his notes for his novel two floors above, or even his own life. Only the baby kittens.

Who could abandon such a man? This was the kind of person my husband was, strange, loving, lethal. He had rescued the kittens. He was prepared to give his everything to do it. But now, on my retreat, I understood: He had also almost killed them.

I gotta stop him, I thought at last.

Here's what I thought: He really needs to be dead.

And that was not long after we went to the colorful party and I found my new friend.

Surely I wasn't actually going to make it happen? (On *Oprah,* from the women's wing of a maximum security facility, on a Mitsubishi forty-inch set wheeled onto the ABC stage, I could say I suffered from obsessive-compulsive disorder and twist my hands constantly, or from multiple personality disorder and call myself "her.")

I made contact with somebody who could help me at least think about getting him killed. I don't want to say, here, where I found this person. You know I had no friends left. That I had met one new person, at the party. I phoned an unlisted number, spoke in code, made a date, wrote it in my calendar as "busns meetng w/ K."

PART II

17

The killer and I met in a Thai restaurant filled with fish tanks. The four tanks were azure, sparsely inhabited, brilliant, the only light source in the room. He looked to be in his late twenties and was, as you know, tall and glum. He was wearing a black jacket that hung on his shoulders as if from a hanger; his sleeves were too short, and from them protruded skinny wrists and truly big hands. His face was furtive and intelligent under contemporary hair that stood straight up. He was so clean shaven his cheeks looked powdered. He was, frankly, just adorable. He sat still in the glowing darkness and said in a low voice that he would be willing to kill my husband in the middle of a weekday night (Saturday nights were less good because of all the people in the street, and anyway he went out of town on weekends, to his former girlfriend's parents' house on Shelter Island), by climbing in the southern-most bedroom window if I would leave it raised one inch

("That's the one to use, right? Or how bout the doors you mentioned from the garden?"

"They're nailed."

"Meaning what?"

"They're . . ." He was right: What did it mean? Our house was nailed shut! "The french doors happen to be nailed," I said finally.

"Yes. But for what reason?"

"They just — they were already that way when I came. I'm not sure why."

"Maybe to prevent a murderer getting in the house."

"Hey look," I said. "It's not your business. It's *our house*. Just climb in the window!") — he'd do it by strangling.

We drank a bottle of chardonnay with our satay and pad thai, my heart settled in my chest, and the killer turned back into a cranky sexy young guy who was writing a novella and had graduated from Reed. I could smell his skin — a clean spicy scent, sort of like a geranium. I told him, "I'm not really planning this. I'm just meeting you for information. I wouldn't really do something like this."

"Then don't."

"But I'm almost — I don't know — afraid to *not* do it."

He said, "Your hand is amazingly cold. It's amazing. Look, don't do anything. If this is wrong for you, I'll be happy to've had a restaurant meal and spent time with a lovely if overly tense woman, and I'll stroll home to the Slope perfectly content. It's a great night for a walk. Don't give it a thought."

He reached for his water glass, and I jumped. But he only sipped, the goblet so level the ice didn't clink. Delicately, he set it down, like a dancer hitting a mark. No fuses blew. Nothing splashed, shattered, bled, or burst into flame. This is what I had come to: impressed that a man could set a glass on a table.

I began to be lulled into — not sleep, not nearly, but a gliding resting state. My panting stopped. So I had been panting! "How old are you?" I asked.

"Thirty in October."

"You look younger."

"I'm not."

"How tall are you?"

"Six one."

"Really?"

"I 'look shorter'?"

"Well, are you really that tall?" I remembered my husband! The killer was the same height as my husband! My dear husband was still with us! Nothing had changed! I panted again until my fear subsided.

My husband weighed more, but the killer was experienced, whereas, I realized, my husband was in some way utterly without crucial information. Also I imagined the killer to have an innate feeling for the ways of enlisting in his own cause the weight and strength and zeal of the opponent, of making those his own. Struggle with him and you'd braid yourself paralyzed. Rush in his direction and you'd wipe yourself out.

"My husband used to box, a little."

"That's fine."

Maybe he and I could run away together? Behind his spiky smart-looking head, a lone Siamese fighting fish reversed course and twitched past. The killer shifted in the gloom and watched me. He said, "Uh-oh."

"What?"

"I have to explain something. It's delicate, but let's just say it. What you're feeling doesn't mean much; it's, y'know, a part of the process, and you'll recover fast — pretty soon after we finish, the feeling goes away. It's like with the doctor, or the shrink. It's like a — what's it called? — shipboard romance. Basically, it's transference. People always fall in love with the hit person. He's going to save their life."

"I'm not in love with you," I said. "I'm — deciding. I'm — relaxed."

"I know more about this than you do."

"You and I are not lovers! There's no way I love you! Those are not my feelings! I do not feel those things!"

"I'm not sure I believe you."

"Well, *believe it.*"

Then we waited again, while the Thai waitresses stood with their backs pressed against fancy wallpaper, hoping for our speedy departure; and the single Siamese fighting fish trailed disconsolately back and forth, looking for the mate it couldn't share a tank with because they'd tear each other to shreds; and my mind produced, instead of thoughts, a field of whitish haze. At eighteen, the killer had written his first novel, in ten weeks. He had coughed it up like a furball and it had been published by Knopf. His new novella was going to be a technical tour de force: In every sentence, some word was going to be out of place; you wouldn't notice it but you'd become unnerved. For a young man, what a grooved, overinformed face he had, how pessimistic! — as I suppose befitted a practitioner of his two professions. "I do want to get him killed," I said finally. He said — tactfully, forbearingly, because by now we were close — "I know that."

He glanced at the waitress, who rushed over to take his resigned order for more glasses of wine. He told me that women have one certain thing in common with men and one thing only: They're mammals. He told me that the commonest masculine interpersonal style is an avoidant one, not punitive but desperate, a style looked down upon, hated, and pitied by women the world over. He told me that if men and women were different species, men would be considered a secondary, primitive, deeply inferior one. He was darling! He reminisced in passing about his harrowing, bookish, alcohol- and blood-soaked childhood in unfortunate Baltimore. Then he took my camera away from me and set it on the table, accepted my brown lunch bag containing my preliminary good-faith one thousand dollars, and took my hands in his. He said, "From what you're indicating, this guy used to give you a hot beef injection three times a week, and obviously you once dug that."

How offensive. I smiled sweetly.

"Most probably," he said, "you still love him — no, don't say anything. Let's stipulate that you do. But what I'm saying, really what you're telling me and I'm paraphrasing, is: He's dangerous. Whatever he may look like — nice guy, industrious guy, good with dogs, formulates clever analogies, whatever — you have to realize, and you *are* realizing, you *have* realized, that your husband is armed and dangerous. If you take no action, eventually, probably not this week but probably soon, he is going to take you down. He doesn't know it, but he *has to* do that. It's in him. So from some standpoint, we can see that this guy, your husband, he's a serious menace to himself too. He's bent on destruction. When things reach this point, you're out on a limb together and he's gonna saw the limb off.

"Right so far?" he said.

"I don't know."

"Let's correct it where it's wrong."

I said, "It's not wrong."

We were examining each other's eyes. His appeared black. He said, "The most important part is, we'll wait for you to decide. We'll do that together. You be sure. If it takes months, fine. If it takes years, just fine. You and I will be waiting as long as it takes."

In the ladies' room, on the toilet, obviously somewhat drunk, I leaned my head against the side of the stall. Peeing was taking forever. I wanted to get back to see his morose pretty face again, see him sitting still in the darkness, hear the low voice and find out what came next. Everything was too slow: hot wind of the wall-mounted dryer nozzle, muscling the door open, down a hall, across indoor-outdoor carpet past the fish environments with their miniature fronds swaying, back to the table with its lavender tablecloth stiff with an excessive proportion of synthetic fiber. I sat, and he gave me a doctorly glance. He said, "Okay?"

"Yes."

"So. You want to hear the rest?"

"Yes."

"You do?"

"Yes." And then, as I had said to dear Dennis, who wanted to talk about Goffman, the first time we met: "Tell me."

The killer said, "Now. One caveat. I'm assuming you've tried your every try and you walked into a wall."

Had I tried my every try?

"You feel implicated. Right?"

"I am," I said.

"Right. You are. Ever and always. Have you gone beyond the ordinary squabbles and threats and betrayals and partings and rethinkings and reconciliations and heart-to-hearts and general sturm und drang? My premise is you have."

"Not the partings," I said.

"Whoa. Back up. You've never separated?"

"No."

"Not for a month or two, to think it over?"

"I went for one week. I had an assignment. We weren't 'separated.' Never for a month. He says we can't."

" 'He says we can't,' " the killer said. "This is important. You can't leave him, right? There's no way you could leave him?"

"I drove up to Provincetown," I said dopily. "I sat on my bed in the rain. The only good part was that I saw *Jurassic Park* again."

"You're kidding. Racism and woman-hating and cruelty to children and cruelty to fat people and piles of shit and snot on peoples' faces and boy games — this is the movie you enjoyed? That's really stupid."

"Obviously you saw it also," I said irritably. "Could we finish what we're talking about? I'm getting exhausted."

"Sure. It's just so idiotic, the movie you went to. Okay. So this is a situation where there's no trial separation permitted. Right?"

"It's more extreme than that."

"Definitely," he said. "It always is. But are we in the ballpark?"

"Yes."

"So let's go with my customary spiel and we'll see, okay? Here it is. Have you done everything you can imagine and he's still like having a live grenade around the house? Have you determined that there's no way you can leave him? Because, needless to say, if you can leave him and everybody survives, that's why we've got divorce. But Raoul Felder usually gets those calls. I don't get those calls."

"Is Raoul Felder a divorce lawyer?"

"A fine and expensive one. I'm assuming this is not a case for Raoul. Is it?"

I thought for a long time. I swallowed most of my glass of chardonnay. I said, "No."

He said, "You don't hire me because you're tired, and you don't hire me because you fell out of love or got sick of the guy, or if there's anything you could possibly do. Needless to say — but I'll say it now — this is a relationship. It's half your problem. If you can imagine making a case that it's not precisely fifty-fifty, call Raoul."

"Could you explain this a little more?"

"Look. Look at it this way, because believe me this is always what it comes down to: One of you has to be stopped. You've shown a nice lively instinct for self-preservation. You've decided it's gonna be him."

"Oh no." Oh, horrible. I flashed him a big inappropriate grin.

He said, "My suggestion is, don't permit yourself at this point to go to any extremes. Don't get overly pumped up. Don't get enmeshed in a whole lot of self-criticism — that's a diversion. And hey, y'know? This isn't just happening at your house; it's rampant."

"This is why there are so many divorces?" I asked sweetly, now utterly drunk.

"*No.* This is why we have the expression 'My wife doesn't understand me.' This is why perfectly capable women go around saying, 'I wish his plane would crash.' "

"Hey! I said that!" What a happy moment. He had retroactively read my mind. I awarded him another of my best, wettest smiles.

"I'm sure you did," he said. "I'm assuming you said all the stuff that wives say."

"When he lies on the couch I picture him with a tag on his toe!" I confessed, and I laughed brayingly.

"Right. That's attractive of you. And this is why I need a beeper. This is why I get a new unlisted number every four months. This is why my stupid telephone rings off the hook."

With the confused intentness of the inebriate, I was thinking about the way he was holding my fingers, which I now considered to be a major caress. His touch seemed so unfamiliar not only because I didn't know him but because it was unvarying — his hot dry hands cradling mine, no more slackly or urgently at any point in his remarks than in the recent reunion moment, after the ladies' room, when, disoriented, I had found the table and dropped myself into my seat and he had taken my hands. He said now, "You seem to need a tremendous amount of reassurance. I think this is the longest speech I've ever made. But it's almost finished.

"So. When this is done — next week or the week after, or next year — I'm leaving over the garden wall and you and I are not gonna see each other again. Buy my book. But, on the night we'll choose, you open the window and we're gonna do this together and we're gonna know, together, what we need to know about your motivation. Here's what it is: self-defense."

He smiled the saint's smile, sorrowful, detached, as though reaching his healing hand into the troubled situation from a vast and ancient distance. On the sidewalk a few minutes later we would fall silent and hug in farewell, and I would lay my cheek against his shirtfront, smelling starch, feeling heat. In the photograph I took that night, the killer is much more vivid and solid than he ever was in the restaurant booth; his satiny cheeks are broader, his eyes are black, and neon tetras appear to be streaking into his ear. The picture lies, but I have it still, framed in a traveler's case. Much later, at night, when I was on the road, even in the roar of semis it opened with an audible click.

18

We met again. He stopped over in the afternoon, wearing a meter reader's I.D. card with his picture on it, to memorize the layout. Dennis was at the library for the day. We ran it through: the killer's approach along the sidewalk in a dorky sports jacket and student's wire-rimmed glasses; his right turn into the alley alongside the east side of the house; around to the back, over the wall, and through the iron gate (left open by me); use the ladder leaning against the pile of bricks; a little quiet scramble onto the roof of the porch; in the window, fast; fast toward Den's side of the futon, quick light dancing steps across the rose-colored rug. At this point we stopped. The killer didn't touch the bed. We stood side by side. Together we looked down at the king-size pillow where Den's condemned head would lie.

Ran it through again, including his escape.

Ran it through again.

Ran it through again.

Then we went outside, and I served some iced tea, and a sherry for me. Midafternoon sherry, what an excellent idea. The early-summer garden was already overgrown, a shaggy green room with foliage walls, crab apple branches bumping the rhododendrons, grass too high. The killer and I sat in the rustling. He carefully sipped, his ice clinked musically, he soundlessly set down his glass. After a long and what I considered to be a resonant pause, filled with interesting traffic noise, he said, "Delicious tea. I like the way you floated this excessive number of mint leaves in it. You want to meet one more time before we off Dennis?"

"I'd probably feel better if we did," I admitted.

He said, "Me too," and held my hand.

We met in the Cajun place for a late-morning lunch. Huddled in arctic chill and restaurant dusk, we scarfed up a mountain of deep-fried crayfish with stabs of our forks. We were the only customers, alone with our grease-streaked platter. The waiter concealed himself in the kitchen. I drank two beers.

Then, beginning tentatively, in increasingly urgent self-justification I constructed an incomplete but otherwise true portrait of Dennis — the spilling, the lurching, the shattered furniture, the bone breaks, the tears. In the interest of clarity, I suppressed any news of Den's kindness, his sweetness, his almost never bearing a grudge. I talked at length. The killer said "Yes" about a hundred times. What a splendid listener. He had heard it all before. He said, "It's infantile, huh? No developed comprehension of spatial relationships. No consideration of their effect on people." I talked more. My fear. The true impossibility of leaving — this I couldn't prove, but with every part of me I knew it. The restaurant seemed to drop further into darkness. The waiter didn't come. Still I jawed on.

"He's dyspraxic," said the killer. "Guy can't plan his physical moves."

Yes! My husband doesn't understand me! And I don't understand him! And he can't plan his physical moves! I wish his plane would crash! Thinking it might be fetching, I murmured, "I feel . . . savage."

The guy did have a tendency to be excessively poetic. He told me, "Hyenas are born with a full set of teeth. The first thing they do in the world is try to kill their littermates."

I snapped, "So what?" Of course I was under a lot of strain.

He laughed. "So your littermate has become an intractable problem."

Two days later, while I was alone in the garden taking pictures of the wall, he came around the house and touched my shoulder. "How did you know I was here!"

"Are you kidding? I'm watching the house. I'm not a random passerby. I'm a murderer." He grinned gloomily.

"I like your hair all yanked back in clips like that. You look harried but quite lovely."

I blushed. I snapped his picture.

"Got any tea?"

I snapped three more.

"Whoa. Very masculine. Maybe you're too strung out and I should leave."

I could feel myrtle against my ankles, and the camera's weight, which I never feel. My underpants were wet. He was standing extremely still, which, if you've been married to Dennis, could make you come on the spot.

"So. Ms. Freakout. You gonna have some ice tea with your pal the hired gun?"

"I'm very entitled to be nervous," I said.

"Maybe talk together like we used to? Converse about this and that? Maybe discuss events in the actual, outside world?"

"You're not funny. It's not cute."

"Yes or no?"

"Okay, yes."

"So I should take a seat?"

"Sure. Fine. Fine. Absolutely. Sit right down."

In late June we suddenly had days of warm wind, blueness, golden light, and people walking ecstatically around the city in a bliss of weather.

Passing the park, I saw the killer sitting on a stone bench, listening to a young woman. She kept rising as if to leave, but then, over and over, she sat down again.

After that I couldn't sleep for three nights. Sharp black nights with stars, three crescent moons rising.

The next Monday I was near the register at the grocery store and he got in line behind me, carrying three packages of oatmeal cookies. It was too bright in here, light flashing off the salad bar, the cucumber rounds and watermelon chunks and chickpeas glistening alarmingly. My nerves were shot. "Quit following me," I said.

"Whoa," he said pleasantly, before departing without a further word. Then for a week I rushed out to that store twice daily, embarrassing myself before the entire intelligent watchful Korean family, until (the father looking out the window crying, *"Your friend coming!"*) the killer finally showed up.

Like a bridal couple, we set a date.

Fourth of July weekend. Quiet streets, anybody who could leave the city gone; the three of us alone.

The morning after our decision I rose slowly out of a sulfurous sleep, wondering, What are we? What are we? Just little animals that need to fall unconscious every twenty-four hours in order to even keep living. I had been dreaming I was making a perilous climb: I was the lover of a billboard painter, visiting him on the scaffold.

19

The day I had scheduled for the death of my husband dawned early and suddenly, with a lucid blue sky. Fourth of July and already hot before the sun cleared the rooftops. The night of the third, Dennis had called me twice to come to bed but then subsided. I had lain awake and watchful on the daybed through the long hours of dark. When the bright and fatal day broke, I was already standing in Dennis's study, peering through cracks between the diagrams obscuring his former view, trying to get what seemed my final glimpse of the river and, beyond it, Manhattan gleaming gold.

Morning stretched ahead, a blue and endless sea. Dennis woke and staggered to his study, already beginning to compose. At ten there was a crash, and my heart twitched — only a wastebasket being kicked, and then, in one of Den's stupendous domino effects, a standing lamp toppling, followed by books spilling themselves off the shelves and a table going down.

I smiled a grim and silent smile. I walked through the house in a dream of neatness, folding laundry, polishing silver, aligning chairs; Den would breathe his last on starched sheets, and when the NYPD arrived, the house would look really great, like a place of true shelter. I consulted my watch so many times it started to appear to be a martian object, radiating UFO strangeness. I took pictures of our home inside and out, eight rolls of color film, long views and closeups. Light against a door frame. Nuthard peaches in a bowl; they'd ripen after Den was under ground. The sofa. Its cushions. Was I already planning to redecorate? Ten shots of Den's closed door.

At last my courage rose and, as if normally, I left the house. Walked down the broiling sidewalk with an exaggeratedly ordinary preoccupied look on my face. The excursion started to take on a life; I warmed to my task and initiated jovial stressed-out hot-weather conversation with passersby. I walked to the supermarket, where I stood a long time at the deli counter, watching the slicer, the gleaming slices of provolone folding off the blade. The butcher called my number and I started.

I bought a tremendous ham. A giant could kill another giant with it. I lugged it home and scored its fat into diamond shapes and stuck it full of cloves and poured Madeira and cider over it (I drank some of the Madeira) and set it into the oven under a tent of foil. This took one hour. Who would eat the ham? you ask. Me, when I was widowed? Den, when he was dead? Aha! No! Think about it! This was an alibi! What woman scheduled to kill her husband would spend the afternoon baking a ham that would serve twenty-five? Then it occurred to me that the police detective, with his slow but deadly Columbo intuition, might wonder about the cast of mind of a woman who had invited no person to share the ham, and who thought in the first place that a ham was the typical American Independence Day food and ought to be baked on a one-hundred-degree day. (Maybe it was! Maybe hams were being set out on picnic tables at this moment all over this vast country! This was a momentarily distracting issue, impossible to resolve and mercifully fleeting.) I stood awhile, soaked with sweat from my exertions, thinking hard. I tried picturing a crowd of guests at our table, their faces bright and dark in the chiaroscuro of the candlelit dining room, ham steaks before them, some starry wintry night. No, it's fine, I thought, and left the big pink thing in the oven.

Anxiety rising.

To quell it, I ascended to the third floor, ran a tepid bath, got into the tub to try, at least, to cool my skin — maybe I could settle down from the outside in. I could hear boats on the river and wind in the trees, could hear Bianca thinking her frog thoughts three stories down. I was going to get him finished off and I would be safe and free (and rich) and my life would start. Wet hair clung to my forehead, my body was feverish, and inside I was growing cold with swelling fear and new grieving.

Den came out of his room and knocked on the bathroom door while opening it, hurting his knuckles. He smiled nicely, displaying traces of cheesy bagel from three hours before. He said, "Sweetheart, I smell cooking. Don't cook, it's too hot. I'll take you out tonight for something you'd like to eat. What would you like to eat?"

"Oh," I said.

He sat on the edge of the tub, balanced so precariously I could see he might fall on top of me, knock me under, and drown me. Even Den — even a blind man — could see something was wrong. "What is it?" he said. "What, what?"

I closed my eyes and let myself slip under the water, stalling, but when I ran out of breath and emerged, he was staring at me closely, more closely, as I recall it, than Dennis had ever looked at me in all the time I knew him. Gazing intently and mindlessly, like a dog watching its owner emerge from a pond. "What's wrong?" he was already saying as I broke the surface.

"Nothing. I'm hot."

"You look sort of sick."

"I'm —"

"Are you sick?"

"I don't," I said, "feel good." I didn't, either. I felt so ungood it was without precedent. I felt terrible beyond describing.

He, my nice husband, the future dead man, jumped up, slipped, cracked his elbow on the sink, flung open the medicine cabinet, and rooted among dental floss and ointments. "I'm looking for —" he said over his shoulder. "Maybe you need —" he said. "You seem to be —"

He scrabbled through vials of pills that had lost their potency years before he and I ever met. He turned and faced me again, where I hung Biancalike in slowly cooling and graying water. "Are you feeling —? What are you —?"

Well, Dennis knew something. How he knew it, I couldn't have said, nor would I have believed in advance that he could've begun to recognize something like this ever in his lifetime. He didn't have the sensitivity for it, the psychic tools, the attention span. Yet he knew. Strings of wet hair obscured my view of my husband as he stood riveted in his own posh bathroom, clutching useless tiny bottles, still as the often-mentioned deer in headlights. Anxiety thumped in my ears. I saw my hideous self laying him, rouged, into the satin bed he would sleep in forever with bottles of amoxicillin still gripped in one meaty frozen hand. He moved toward the bath and perched on the edge again (this time gracefully, but how could that be? yet there it was, a graceful sitting), and he told me, "Sweetheart, you don't have to say a word. I can see that something is bothering you. And I just want you to know I'll help you any way I can. You tell me what it is, and believe me, honey, it can't be as bad as you think. And we can work on this together. We can. You don't worry. I see it's something bad. But we can fix it."

Sympathy overcame me, floods of it, and then a devastating sense of timelessness in which these feelings could never end. Outside, the summer sun was still high. We had not even begun to approach anything like nightfall. Passionately, Den reached into the water and crushed my hand in his. Tears of unfocused tenderness welled in his eyes, and in mine. The wintry aroma of Vermont ham rose from the kitchen through ninety-degree air.

Only a sort of monster could live with this man. But only a metamonster could hate him. And at last, stiff with confusion, lying underwater like a miserable bottom-feeder, my wrinkled fingers crunched in his smooth ones, of course I finally understood: I could not have my husband killed.

The evening flew and it went on forever. Ham sandwiches. Our ascent to the roof to watch the fireworks over the river. Den's tripping on the tar paper and almost falling into the street to his death, my reflexive grab at his shirt, his miraculous achievement of equilibrium. The deep thudding booms, then the flowers bursting into bloom above the city, the sprays of light spilling into black water. Our descent without mishap.

I had thought a long time about how to say good-bye, and in the bedroom as we turned out the light, I said it just in case. "We've had our differences, but I have to say you've been a real husband to me. In most ways you've been a better partner than I have." Of course it was true. I wanted him to know I knew it. He nodded, looking extremely stupid.

Dennis slept at once, sweating and still. I waited four hours minute by minute, in darkness, heat, sounds of fire-crackers like distant gunfire, snores human and canine, ticking, for the moment when the killer would be opening the gate and I would be slipping down the stairs and into the garden to give him his money and tell him I'd changed my mind. Den lay as if already slaughtered, posthumously drooling. He stirred, patted at my thigh, and dropped into deeper sleep. He smelled like mustard.

At three I got up and dialed Jane in Kentucky, who I knew was away, just to hear her recorded voice and her beep. I tiptoed downstairs and ate breakfast by candlelight, two English muffins, heavily buttered to help them slide down.

I went out the front of the house into steamy moonlight and walked around to the back. The street was empty. The garden in the middle of this night was a rustling magic place, a Romeo and Juliet place, and I was awaiting my Romeo, the one I deserved. I waited.

Precisely at four, of course, the killer dropped over the wall into the garden, his straight-up hair spiky against the street lamp's light, sneakers soundless, eyes bright. He stepped onto the patch of grass, turned to be sure the gate stayed open, turned back, and saw me sharing the garden with him in my sleepwalker's nightdress. The haze was clearing fast, like a roof lifting, and stars were popping into the predawn sky. All around us, white blossoms bloomed in the dark.

We looked at each other. We each took a step.

"What?" he whispered. "What is it? What?"

PART III

20

I ran.

I released the killer from his obligation and drove him home. I held his strangler's hands and thanked him with tears in my eyes. I fled that night.

The moon roof open — wind and stars. Dawn sky rushing overhead. Seized with wild joy.

Why pretend I hadn't planned it? Certainly I left behind almost everything: my cameras, tripod, precious negatives, books, pictures, CDs, rolling papers, note-books, dress shoes, periodontist's receipts; the gold vel-vet daybed, the striped chair I'd flown right over when Dennis threw me across the room, the empty refrigera-tor humming day and night for the purpose of storing the cold air it produced; my Rolodex, containing the numbers of all the people I'd once thought I knew; the record of our marriage in photographs, unfinished — finished now; the lovely nacreous bathtub, which was already, in the instant I drove away, beginning to glow in my memory like a cradle of mother of pearl; my ravenous, silent childhood and the grief it had occasioned — the very grief that had heretofore destroyed my every romance until inevitably it brought me to my last chance, the moment in which I decided to marry Dennis. And I left Raleigh. And my crutches; and my van; and my vivid, angry, confused, unmurdered husband.

I took: his car.

And I took: the frog.

Trembling and racing, in any moment of flight, you believe you can leave your life behind. Motel just outside the city. I fell across a queen's bed as dawn traffic was beginning to hum, slept like an adolescent until afternoon, left the air conditioner blowing and ate at Mickey D's, returned to motel, air cigarettey and cold, washed grease off chin with small pink perfumey soaps. I fell dead asleep and woke hours later, dazed, amnesiac, and refreshed.

Foreign motel world; that other world, back at the house, not yet gone. I was quite fascinated by the faux wood-grain television console, plastic glasses wrapped in plastic film, dead flies trapped behind tweedy curtains, coruscating motel shag. I opened a drawer to check out the Bible and flyswatter. Feeding Bianca her frog bites, checking her water temp, I stared into the bucket as if into tea leaves, but she silently screamed to have the lid slapped back on.

Then I dialed.

I told the machine I was fine, perfectly safe, only not myself, only in critical need of time away, and I'd call again, sooner than later, when I could, and I hung up fast. It seemed to me that my deciding to murder my husband, deciding not to murder him, stealing his car, stealing his pet, driving away from our shared home in the night after giving a freelance killer a lift to Park Slope, and formulating a plan and promise to telephone "when I could" — all of this seemed, under the circumstances, entirely prudent, moderate, apt. With tenderness and grim amusement, I imagined Dennis, even now, back in Brooklyn with all the lights on, plunging from room to room, packing both clean and dirty clothes, finding his jacket under the couch, provisioning for the journey during which he would try and try and finally fail to recover his lost wife.

Bianca and I checked out at six at night, in vibrant daylight. Where were we going? We were going in silence. I reached behind me to stroke Raleigh's head, but of course he wasn't there. Holding, instead, the handle of Bianca's bucket, I headed, randomly, north.

21

Demons at our backs, we gave the frisky Alfa its head. Two travelers, one of them sloshing in a bucket, one accelerating and shifting and planning for two, fled the bandages and the bloodstains and the chronic air of menace, the nailed-shut french doors, the convoluted perorations, the lives she and I had effortfully tried to live in basement and above. Bianca under her lid was a surprisingly comforting presence. Out here on the road, fleeing with the frog, I felt, for the first time in a year, accompanied.

As it happened, Bianca and I, solitary runaways amphibious and human, were not, at the moment, strictly speaking, on our own — we were part of a traveling community. Already the Alfa drivers were spotting us and waving — perky wimpy Spyder Veloces, new Fiats in Alfa clothing, even the sedate arriviste sedans. Barreling ahead in the beefy GTV, we were Alfa Romeo royalty, and, as is the case with royals generally, we were always

being watched. At home, unmoored; on the road, an-
chored.

Outside the car, bright fields in dazzling heat. Soon
we would leave New York State, and in a few hours we'd
approach Canada and would stop for the night —
wouldn't we? Here's how I was thinking. We had left
our Brooklyn, frog and I, by mutual silent agreement.
We had come this far in tacit concord, never mentioning
what we were doing, where we were headed, how we'd
know when we arrived. You know this thing wasn't
solved. But why think now? Time to move. We pumped
some gas and kept going. And now a country road was
sliding under us and we were sneaking into the rocky
but welcoming state of Vermont in our stolen car.

If I had actually got Dennis killed, even indolent
cooping cops would've nabbed me and Bianca by now,
because we were limping. Half an hour into Vermont, I
grew queasy. I turned off the air conditioner, opened the
windows, let hot air blow in. We were on back roads in
picturesque country — deep green, lavish woods and
voluptuous hills — when I started having to intermittently pull over, clutch a towel, and try to vomit. Well, as
you know, I had been under major stress. Of course one
becomes nauseated!

In front of an antiques store in a silent eighteenth-
century town, I stopped to crouch on the curb. "I'll
be okay!" I yelled toward the car. "I'll just barf and then
I'll come right back!" Through the store window you
could see they were hawking the customary Depression-
era radios, oak pigeonhole desks, marcasite brooches,

Japanese salt and pepper shakers, horrible cookie jars representing the stupid heads of fat red-lipped children — it was a dispiriting array in any case, and actively depressing to a sick person on the lam. I yelled, bravely, inaccurately, "I'm almost finished!"

Across the street a small ancient man sat on his porch gazing at me — apparently into my eyes, though why would this geriatric jerk, as I now identified him, seek to share a lover's glance? "I'm coming, babe!" I hollered at my car. The old man was half obscured by the American flag hanging from his porch roof (it was sort of a Robert Frank image), and he peeked around its stripes to observe my struggle with nausea as though he had bet serious money on the outcome. I had the distinct impression that the lower I sank the more he would collect. Occasionally a roaring truck downshifted through town, breaking the staring contest the old guy and I were maintaining as I sweated and reeled curbside. "Couple more minutes, Bianca! Be right there!" The breeze picked up and some postcards slipped off a table and arranged themselves at my feet — Yosemite, Monticello, Las Vegas, New Orleans, Niagara Falls, Death Valley, every American playground. Oh froggie dear but we are far from home.

A truck ground by; the old man, my nemesis, disappeared behind it; water flooded in my mouth. I yelled "One more minute!" and threw up on the sidewalk. He reappeared. He looked really pleased — ready to cash in. I gave him the finger. Then we drove on.

*

"We have to stop," I told her. The next place was a Victorian hotel offering many types of seating — painted rockers lining a deep porch, rattan settees, Adirondack chairs on a sweep of lawn. An ordinary person might stop and think here. Any person, even one afraid to think and toting a medium-size bucket and many boxes of soft frog pellets (hard foods cause internal damage), could vanish here. Nobody would find her.

I slept, in my T-shirt and jeans, on the chintz spread. At night, when the heat had lifted and all the other guests — the normal guests, with their potent sunscreens and white trousers and human companions — were dining out, I woke, expecting Dennis and Raleigh and Brooklyn. The room was black. Bianca waited. I changed her water, tossed her some nibbles, went to the bar and drank two Cokes, and slept for ten more hours.

When I woke at noon, we left the inn, to save our money (we had a lot of Dennis's cash, but we also might be making an exhaustive trip), and drove for twenty minutes. At the Moonlighter Motel outside Dorset, the man in the office greeted us with a look of unshakeable pessimism. I lay down on an Early American sofa with several heartbreaking doggy pulls in it, to await the subsiding of new nausea so Bianca and I could check in. From my prone position, without moving my lips I asked, "Will we like the room?"

"You got somebody with you? You didn't ask for a double."

"I mean will *I* like it."

"We don't get too many complaints. Truthfully, we don't hear too much about the rooms one way or the other. Would you want to look at it?"

"I'm not feeling very well. Just tell me."

"Waaal, y'know, honestly, it's a motel room."

"Do the windows open?"

"Honestly? Not too well." He gazed at me wondering as I reclined on my bed of pain. Fuck him — he's never seen a nauseated woman on the run with a frog? I let my bored eyes fall shut. While enjoying a nice long silent rest, I heard the man's voice ask if I wanted the room, because he needed to go out and truthfully he couldn't have me lying on the couch for the rest of the —

Guy with attitude. "How's the availability of rooms around here right now?" I rallied and inquired.

"Slim pickins, really."

"If you were me, would you be optimistic about finding a room where you can open the windows, farther up the road?"

"If I was *you,*" he said, "I wouldn't be sure of makin' it to the car."

Struggling inaudibly on the motel sofa, I probably did not appear to be a fugitive. I probably looked like what I was: a married woman who didn't know where she was going. The motel guy shuffled around the desk to straighten his rack of pamphlets, with an eye to getting a closer gander at me and my bucket. I glared at the guy until he slunk back to his post. I covered my eyes with my hand. I said I'd take the room.

"One bed okay?"

"Of course!" I snapped. "There's only me!"

"Jeez, I'm just double-checking. You got your own way of doing things, I glean."

"I'm not traveling with another person!"

The motel guy, with impressive focus, jingling the key: "'At's okay. I'm not the sheriff, neither."

Inside the motel room I slept, and dreamed:

I wake in sunlight with the sound of the shower running, and the killer comes out of the bathroom with his wet hair standing straight up. He sits next to me — next to us, actually, since the bucket is naturally in the bed. He's wearing a tannish (flesh-colored) shirt, with a frayed sleeve whose edge I finger tenderly. Morning light streaking the room. I can hear Raleigh panting outside the door, and soon I'll go out and hug his matted neck. The killer holds *my* neck in his hands as he would've held Den's immediately before snuffing the life out of him — Is Dennis dead and gone? I'm afraid he must be. The killer keeps his hands, hot, around my throat.

Next, the killer and I — in our several motel beds, in the car at Mickey D's with the old man observing, standing together slippery with suds on the sandpapery petal-shaped fall-prevention decals in a molded plastic tub — the killer and I are having the erotic time of our lives. We are fucking in dry air and wetness! In an aquamarine swimming pool, we dip ourselves, then slide to our secret room.

Afternoons in bed, nights driving under cover of darkness, avoiding arrest and looking for breakfast. We're hiding out — Dennis can't kill us. I like it safe inside our outlaws' car. Days pass between meals; then we eat eggs and toast and jam, and glug down enough coffee to last awhile. Raleigh is with us and we're all tremendously hungry. We buy gigantic hamburgers. We're heading toward something. We will not meet a good end. I keep track of the money and he keeps filling the tank.

Hunger woke me. Outside, summer rain. I felt surprisingly well. Before dawn in our motel room, which smelled like ointment, I swam up from sleep, recalling:

Den, in a rage: "You don't like Raleigh."

"Don't be silly."

"You don't."

"Of course I do."

"I can tell you do *not*."

"Dennis, I like Raleigh."

"Enough to glad-hand him. Enough to give him the rare condescending pat on the head. Enough to —"

"*Dennis.* I'm not *condescending* when I pat him. He's a *dog*."

"You don't like him. You don't. You don't even try to hide it. You're contemptuous and dismissive about Raleigh!" He had looked so sincerely aggrieved that I laughed, causing him to rush from the room.

After a while I'd found him and tapped his shoulder,

which had heated and moistened his shirt. I nuzzled his radiant neck. "You know I like Raleigh, don't you?"

"You have not made him a part of your family," he muttered.

"I think I welcomed him."

"Grudgingly."

"Not grudgingly. Warmly."

"Effortfully."

Me, laughing: "Effortfully because it's not easy to welcome a dog like him — it *takes* effort. But I did it. I *like* the damn dog." And Den smashed out of the room again, only to return later with a huge bouquet of painted daisies drooping on long stems.

Actually, of course, I had grown to love our dog. I thought of him as mine. I missed him, now, too much. But from Dennis's perspective, my loving Raleigh obeyed only the letter, not the spirit, of some universally respected law governing the human parents of pets. Now, on the road and far from our starting point, I saw what he had meant: real love but not enough.

22

For five days we traveled and did not arrive.

Our seclusion began to grind us down. Bianca ate a lot of frog bites and shed her skin. I phoned home daily to tell the machine a big lie: that we were fine.

At a family restaurant I watched a family — burdened father alone with head-of-household thoughts, over-taxed mother, four rambunctious sons. The mother abruptly handed her pocketbook to the second youngest, her manifest soul mate and favorite, and strolled off to the rest room for a rest.

Immediately my need to confer with a nonamphibian friend was the biggest thing in my hapless life. I left my eggs and my toast triangles soaked with liquid margarine and I followed her like a stalker. She was an awfully ten-derhearted-looking person, with short hair and short legs and a short skirt. In the sanctuary of the ladies' room, soon my new best friend and I were knee to knee on a vinyl couch while I laid the groundwork for telling what was, now I saw, an exceptional story, misshapen and marvelous.

"Do you really have time to talk?"

She sighed. "Definitely."

Prefatorily, I outlined some general thoughts. They had come up in the car. They were apposite for sure, since I was panting with loneliness, and perhaps (as I affirmed I suspected, and as I noticed she did nothing to dispute) she was too. Here's what I told her: Twentieth-century America is a lonely country. American movie stars, we all know, are simply lonely citizens who have been catapulted onto thrones and now employ tasters. But ordinary people too — these days everybody's lonely here: adolescents whether heroin addicts or Whiffen-poofs, young mothers waiting for their children to mature (she liked that part), restaurateurs preoccupied with portion control and spoilage, bank tellers in their cages. Except for Carter, all our recent presidents, not just the sexually rapacious ones, have been horribly lonely — Johnson the loneliest of all. No amount of showing his scar and inviting journalists to watch him take a crap could begin to chip away at Johnson's prodigious loneli-ness. Clinton's loneliness is of course so insistent that he has to assuage it with near-continuous shmoozing and who knows what else —

"That's so true about President Clinton," she inter-rupted to say. Amazingly, my rest-room confidante had retained some interest in our supposed topic.

And, thinking about our own normal, mundane little lives in our own little houses, I felt emboldened to say (I called our two lives "normal" to strengthen our new bond, shrewdly concealing the fact that here our paths diverged fantastically, hers and mine), we can see how loneliness has set the tone. Wasn't *that* true, if you thought about it?

"It really is," she agreed. "I mean, I —"

I would never have married the man I married, I rushed to aver, just as one example that happened to spring to mind, had loneliness not been my constant if then unrecognized companion.

"I probably would've married Roy anyway," she said. "I wanted to have sex with him with a clear conscience. But I get what you mean."

Next she supported me as I left the topics of general loneliness pervasive in the culture and particular decisions individual lonelinesses might seem to mandate, and moved on to thoughts about future action. I affirmed that I still believed that keeping one's commitments is centrally important in life, of paramount significance, after, of course, and it went without saying, nourishment and shelter and survival itself. I said that out here on the road I had been, inevitably — given how I'd gotten here, which was a subtle piece of business in itself upon which I would be delighted to elaborate except that time didn't permit — out here I had been thinking and worrying mile after mile about personal commitment and what it means, that simple, difficult thing. "Uh-huh," she was saying, nodding in predictable but nonetheless comforting sisterhood.

I was so pleased with my rest-room pal. These

thoughts of mine had been developing all this week, inside the aimlessly speeding Alfa. And with my new friend they were playing so well. Her face was gentle and shiny and empathic. Our thighs started sweating and we stuck to the couch. And I continued to express myself.

I omitted, as any sensible person would, the hired-killer section of my narrative. Instead I confessed, "I had fantasies about something happening to my husband."

"Uh-huh, uh-huh!" — now quite animated.

"I imagined his plane might crash."

"Yes! Maybe his car!"

"He wouldn't feel any pain or fear. Right? Some sort of totally painless accident."

"Like he'd just crash his Explorer into a wall and he wouldn't feel one thing."

"Or he'd contract maybe a really quick painless fatal illness?" I suggested. "And he'd succumb with a complete lack of —"

But then she looked at her watch and stood, her legs peeling off the sofa with a ripping sound. "Oh, this is so interesting. I'm glad we talked about this. I hate to leave, but those boys are waiting."

I needed to tell her something more. I held her sleeve and hurried to announce it: "I ran away from home."

She said, in farewell, "I think about it every single day. I'm not kidding you. Not a day passes."

This is what you believe when you're on the road: People can begin anew. Life is a dream.

Still, things were wrong. Bianca and I, so recently embarked in freedom, looked to be heading for a lifetime series of identical rooms outfitted with lamps bolted to the tables, tables bolted to the floor. We zigzagged up and down the back roads, into New Hampshire, back to Vermont, into New Hampshire, from town to delightful town, always staying, with wonderful constancy, the same precise distance from home.

Our next motel room was furnished with lawn chairs and offered a Wake Up Call. Looking to drum up another conversation with a human being, I dialed to request seven o'clock. "Can I depend on that?"

The wake-up man asked, "Why not?"

"I just wanted to make sure because I really need to get an early start."

"So you got it. Seven."

"I need to get on the road, that's all."

"Right. We'll call you."

"I left in a hurry and I didn't pack my alarm clock. This was an unexpected trip so I wasn't totally prepared. But as long as you can —"

"Can what?"

I said, "Wake me."

"We can wake you," he said.

"Great, thanks, so seven A.M., okay?"

"You told me two times already. It's wrote down. We already got the plan to wake you. We're waking you."

"I just wanted to make sure you —"

He said, "I don't know what to tell you, lady. We been doing it for years. We got a clock and we make the calls."

"Great, great. So maybe I could check back with you later to be sure that —"

He hung up.

Unhelpful men are everywhere, pretending to help!

The next night, in a bed-and-breakfast near the Canadian border, I already knew.

All night the gusts from the fan swung across my body like the sweep of a searchlight. I lay listening to trucks on the road, plumbing in the walls, mosquito whine, moths rushing the screen, taps and creaks. Near dawn — just before I slept at last, to enter a place where windows were being shattered by a gale, and to whisper, "Wake me up, wake me" — as I listened my way into sleep, I heard the rag rugs and ladder-back chairs and Early American love seats resting on their waxed warm-colored two-hundred-year-old floorboards; the electric coffeemaker beginning its day; the rows of chenille nubs swirling on the folded bedspread; the crackle of the corn-husk handicrafts pinned to the wallpaper; the clamoring of the many items on the exhaustive things-to-do list on the counter in the kitchen of the house's resourceful landlady; Bianca treading in her bucket-pond in the bathroom, remembering the vegetation of swamps and slow-moving streams; and, from faraway Brooklyn, the sighs of my dangerous, sleeping husband.

At last sleep dropped over me too. I dreamed, of course, of Den. I saw him moistly hugging his pillow, alone in unconscious dishevelment on our bed, and I saw, could see, knew, almost knew, the dreams in his tireless head.

I woke to boiling sunlight again, an oppressive aroma of coffee and chicory, lilting voices of breakfasters below, clack of knives and forks. I descended fast, eager to find, among the faces of those merry oldsters and dazed honeymooners at the table piled with muffins in cozies and jellies in bowls, my husband's face.

I had to go home.

From a lakeside bar featuring strawberry daiquiris, nachos, and potato skins, on a wall phone next to a kitchen staffed by high schoolers, I phoned. He was out, and the phone rang and rang.

23

At a gas station (rusted, picturesque, quintessentially American, of the type that is chronically photographed), I phoned again.

"Hello? Hello? *Hello? Hello?*"

"Den?"

"Okay! Okay okay, hold it! Hold it a minute!" Bumping and clattering. My guess was he had cream cheese on his fingers and was dropping the phone on his foot — still himself and living in Brooklyn. After a while his intense voice came back and said, "There's a cop bulletin out, y'know. You might want to think about that. You're a missing person."

"You've heard from me, Dennis."

"Oh yeah?" — slowly, after a pause, as if stalling.

Was he buying time? Was Harvey Keitel the subtle detective tracing the call, familiar with my past record and suspecting that I was in the grip of a helpless, self-destructive compulsion to drive on? Embarrassed, I whispered, "Is somebody on the other line?"

"*We're* on. I'm on from here and you're on from wherever missing persons live."

"I'm not missing. I may be a lot of things, and I may have made a lot of mistakes, but by no stretch of the imagination can I be considered missing. You have an obligation to tell the police you get phone calls from me and that I'm voluntarily on a trip. You hear from me all the time!"

He chuckled bitterly, choking slightly.

"Are you okay?"

Choking sounds. Background yips from beloved Raleigh.

"*Den. Are you okay?*"

"I'm great," he coughed out. "I'm fine. And you're *[cough]* a missing *[cough]* person."

I said, "You are making the police search for somebody who's not lost. I think you could get in a lot of trouble for that."

He coughed.

"Dennis, I'm positive it's a serious offense to do what you're doing — fooling the police."

"You think 'fooling the police' is what, a felony? or a misdemeanor? You're completely out of it. You kidnapped a frog. FBI is informed also. Uh! Uh! Hold on a minute!" He dropped the phone.

When he came back, in a conciliatory voice I told him my latest hard-won narrative: that I had gone away to think things over, that I'd been extremely confused and needful of solitude and this leave-taking radical though it undeniably was had made sense six nights ago, that I had thought long and hard and in that moment of departure the alternatives I'd been able to envision had not looked promising from anybody's standpoint, mine or his. With intelligent restraint, I passed up the opportunity to specify the alternative I had been planning for myself, that is, prison. And for him, the grave.

And that I was coming home now.

As you know, riding around out in the world had been making me ponder the lives being lived all over this great country of ours. Of course here in America we know that when a married person begins needing regular vacations alone, that married person has a lover. This is an immutable reality. Well, I was not on any vacation. I made that clear. I contrived to tell a reasonable-sounding story of my vivid confusion and amorphous heartache and sudden flight, a story that even to my own ear sounded implausible if not utterly impossible to believe. To the accompaniment of Den's expressive breathing — he was such a strenuous breather it was like having a third party on the line — I spoke at length. I've made mistakes, I was saying. Cut me some slack. After several mannered and tiring paragraphs I fell silent, and we listened awhile to Den's ragged, poignant breaths.

He didn't say, Why had I gone. He didn't say, When would I return. He didn't ask anything about my plans or tell me anything about his. Instead, when at last he spoke, Dennis said, "I'd be curious to know what you think marriage is. If the word 'marriage' has any meaning for you."

What an excellent question! It was elegant — succinct, dignified, painful, and utterly shaming — a beautiful response.

On the highway, trucks blew past. I stood in a hot wind clutching the receiver, trying, against daunting odds, to compose the felicitous answer his query deserved. Nothing would do. Not the intimidated child's "I don't know." Not the political campaigner's "I'm glad you asked." Not the overextended adulterer's "Please don't question me now." After a long, potentially fertile, but finally unproductive silence, I said, "I think when you and I got married we felt we really loved each other."

And canny Dennis said, "I ain't talking about love."

All the way down the Northway, I stared at his question, whose answer, in fact, I knew well. In some admittedly twisted but still, I thought, not entirely dismissable way, of course my idea of marriage was at the center of my original decision to murder Dennis in lieu of divorcing him! I was not so bad! I had married but once; I was an animal that only now, driving home fast, recognized itself: one that marries for life.

Stomping the gas, with equal interest I reviewed remembered moments small and large: Den eating his poppy-seed bagel, distributing one thousand black seeds over the plate, table, chair, rug, floor, then grinning a speckled grin. Den peeling off while I was joining him in the car and dragging me, half in, half out, a quarter block. As Bianca and I drove south, radio music played in the dashboard, but in my busy head images of Dennis were in heavy rotation.

The Northway was filled with cars hectically pressing on toward vacation spots — I hadn't seen families like this in years, the very families we imagine, together, happily encumbered, driving. At rest stops, the families would stand near their campers placidly drinking sodas with an air of having already reached their destinations, as though the point of the vacation were to drive out and picnic in the service area parking lot. Then, with intense resolve, they'd hurl themselves on. What the hell, all the members of my own family awaited Bianca and me, each in his and her singular fashion, one barking, one cowering in the closet, one falling down.

Just as, at home, I had often looked ahead and felt the road under me, now, on the road, I looked back. Across many miles I traveled through air and dropped in from the sky, traveled into Brooklyn Heights, down our expensive street, in the window, looked straight back into my former house, my former life, with the former me in it. We would live it out, he and I. For the last time I was rushing home, the image of Dennis following my car like the moon.

His welcome was operatic, heartfelt, shocking in its intensity, and wet. Drying his eyes, he kitchy-kooed into the bucket. He stood staring with mayonnaise under his nose and a new expression, the haunted look of a man with a single goal: "I am going to make you glad you came home."

"I'm already glad."

And Dennis, with an ardor that caused me a thrill of fear: "Not glad enough. You'll see."

24

By my second morning back, the life of our family had been reconstituted, and we were (to the extent you can do this without sex or epiphanies or soulful bonding or margaritas) experiencing a honeymoon. As a collection of remarkable animals, I thought, our family is incomparable: We bow to no zoo. Icarus in the closet; Bianca in the basement; Raleigh acting as novelist's assistant, scrabbling among wads of paper and nosing them into corners, doing his doggy jobs. Forty times a night, Dennis turned over (up, flips, lands like an exhibition wrestler hitting the mat), and forty times I ground my teeth and renewed my commitment. I lay there like a long-distance trucker, the road sliding in my head. In the morning I woke a self-possessed woman with trembling hands. I set up my tripod and took a shot of myself, with blood all over my nose where Den had clawed me in the night.

*

Day 460: Little Wesley Rolfe, from our third-floor bath-room window, a juggling blur.

Day 461: Above the brick wall, two of Wesley's clubs, one traveling skyward, one dropping fast.

Day 465: From the bathroom again, the green clarity of the Doctors Rolfes' garden, uninhabited. No Wes.

Day 466: Wes's clubs again, twirling in blue!

A young guy on the street said, after Dennis trod on his foot, "Next time, I punch your brains out of your dicking skull," and instantly we were in a fight. Dennis shuffling, feinting and frothing until two gentle muscu-lar good-citizen passersby helped me drag him off the guy.

Saved, Den's antagonist still staggered on the side-walk, glaring. I said to him, "Hey. Please. Quit waving your cape at this man."

Dennis, so glad to have us back, took over the care of Bianca, and soon enough, when I descended to visit her — I was thinking to have a tête-à-tête — she had died.

He had forgotten to change her water, or to keep it warm, or I'll never know what, and now, when I looked in, already formulating the questions I could pose to the frog, there she was, almost precisely the same but utterly, finally changed. Bianca was free-floating in the bucket like a tiny frog balloon. Bianca was pinkish, and Bianca was dead.

It was not only grief dropping over me as I stared into deceased Bianca's last, too-still, too-cold water. Not just sadness. Also fear.

I fled the basement. "Den! Den!" (This was recourse to a bit of theater — he was out, and I knew it.) Then, sotto voce: *"Raleigh. Raleigh. Bianca died."* Raleigh was on the living-room rug, absorbed in genital grooming. He looked at me, before returning to snuffling and biting himself. *"Raleigh,"* I heard myself whisper. *"Dennis killed Bianca. You and I have to leave now. We have to escape."* The dog removed his head from his wet crotch to meet my gaze with curious but moronic canine eyes. I whispered, *"Where's your leash? Raleigh, come on, let's go out,"* and he scrambled up and hustled to the front door, and I considered packing a bag but there wasn't time; the dog was jumping in place and fear was moving me fast. I ran to grab my wallet. And Dennis's key turned in the lock.

He looked to have been hit by a truck. (In fact he had been grazed by a panel truck carrying unsalted pretzels, while he and it were contending for space in a cross-walk.) Seeing his master scuffed and dragging, darling Raleigh jumped straight up in the air. He rushed Den, knocked him down, and pounced, making a repulsive licking sound. "Okay, boy. Okay, boy. I'm okay, boy."

"Bianca died," I said.

From the rug: "What! Bianca? Oh no!"

"Yes. She's dead."

"Why?"

"I think because you didn't dechlorinate the water."

"The water? Oh my god. Are you sure? Of course you're sure. Bianca dead! Oh, how could I forget to fix the water?"

" 'How could you do it.' How do you do *any* of these things? How do they happen?"

"Oh," he squeaked, and he began to cry.

Raleigh stepped on Den's chest and licked his eyes and nose. I sat down next to my heartbroken husband where he lay messily in his pet's turbulent embrace. It smelled muddy and bloody and doggy down here. Poor Dennis seemed the embodiment of — no, the conduit for — something inexorably malignant. I watched the remorseful bloodied face being slavered by the dog. The sweet devoted dog who, I suddenly knew, only momentarily, only fleetingly, but as certainly as I've known anything in my life, would be among the next to go.

Bianca's funeral was celebrated in the back garden by me and Dennis alone — to inter her, we had to lock Raleigh inside so he wouldn't rush to dig her up like a buried fish head. What with his injuries from the pretzel truck collision, Dennis couldn't dig, so I excavated a small lozenge-shaped grave in damp earth while he controlled the volume on some Vivaldi, a supposed favorite of B.'s. I had mounted a black-and-white print, like a nineteenth-century card photograph, promenade or boudoir size, showing Bianca in happier days, in close-up, with the edge of the bucket out of the frame so that she appeared to be floating free in a miniature expanse of silvery sea. Along the bottom edge of the mat (after, roughly, I thought I recalled, the Comtesse de Noailles, buried in Père Lachaise in Paris): "Alas! I can't believe I'm dead!" Wise little Bianca. Irascible sensible little fishy-smelling Bianca. I laid her, my incomparable girl-friend, wrapped in a hand towel, into the earth. When I set her photograph atop the mound, Den understand-ably sobbed like a maniac, clawed his chest, and had to be helped to the house.

In the days after Bianca's passing, Den and Raleigh and I were constantly together, a grieving threesome. At night, gloom and befuddlement kept us sleeping too lightly or watching the ceiling's cracklure. As though normally, Den and I talked in the dark. I was scared of everything we said. Dwelling on Bianca put us in mind of aquatic creatures. Dennis told me about pickerel frogs with orange-colored underparts and common Western frogs: the kinds you can eat. Dennis said he would sauté some soft-shell crabs. He recalled that he had once worked a summer in a sardine packing plant. Sardines are packed by hand. Women snip off their heads and tails with scissors and pack their shining bodies side by side in tins. Dennis and I lay still and hopeless, staring up, two people who could imagine too much about the inner lives of sardines.

In several weeks, Den and Raleigh and I were apart for one moment only. It was the middle of a long night. When it appeared that sleep had finally claimed both dog and man, I slipped the phone out of its charger, crept down the stairs, and stepped into the closet. Icarus the cat was, as usual, curled behind snow boots; I couldn't see her, but my arrival occasioned some tiny cat snorts and purring in the blackness.

I dialed the killer. His number had been disconnected. He was gone.

My former and last hope, vanished. Listening to a dial tone in the sheltering dark of the coat closet, I flushed with a lover's rage, that lover's shock that He's not what he seemed! and How could I have been so wrong? Seduced by my own longing. When, now I seemed to see, this guy was never a murderer after all. He was just one of those men who likes to say yes to women.

Day 473: Bianca's grave. Newly planted myrtle struggling to take hold. Alas, I can't believe I'm dead.

25

Without Bianca I had nobody in the world to talk to. Dennis went back upstairs to his novel, to drown his grief in work. My happiest hours — transiently calm hours, the last I would ever know — were spent walking Raleigh on Joralemon Street, my hand sweating into a plastic dog-poop mitt, my head filled with a sense of borrowed time.

And soon enough, Dennis rose early one morning, left me sleeping off my sleepless night, lured Icarus the cat out of the closet, encouraged her to go out the front door, revved the Alfa and backed out of the alley and absentmindedly ran her over and drove away.

He killed our cat.

Loud talking woke me — citizens gathering, looking at the problem, expressing their thoughts. When I ran out, they perfectly described Den's Alfa Romeo and its wonderful speed, the driver's distracted face with its unseeing eyes. Icarus had bounced. My husband had not noticed.

Two lovely young pierced-tongue women, riddled with silver jewelry but apparently not too hobbled by it, helped me slide Icarus onto a square of cardboard and cover her with a towel. They waved down a cab, and I took the cat, possibly, I hoped, still breathing, to the vet's. My first opportunity to spend some time with her; since the kitchen fire that had rounded off her ear points and devastated her kittenhood, she had been, as I've said, almost entirely incommunicado. I hadn't ever gotten to know her — I had almost never fully seen her — and now Den had run her down.

"I've got a good feeling about this!" the cab driver yelled through bullet-proof Plexiglas and loud sexy salsa. "I think it's gonna pull through!"

"I don't think so!" I yelled.

"You believe it!" he yelled.

I didn't believe it.

Mona, the vet, a known straight shooter, watched me burst in carrying oddly curled and oozing Icarus — dead Icarus, though I was far from prepared to admit that — and said, "He did it again, huh?"

"Can you look at her right away?"

"What'd he do this time, drop-kick her?"

"Who? That's not a very nice thing to say."

Mona carried the orange cat tenderly, laid her down, listened to her heart not beating, and looked at me hard.

"You *are* Dennis's wife, aren't you? We met once at New Year's? Isn't this cat Ginger Girl?"

"Yes. Actually, it's Icarus now. She was Ginger Girl before the fire."

"*Riiight,*" she said. "The *fiiire.*"

"I don't know what you're intimating, but the fire was an accident!"

"So was the last cat he ran down."

Time slowed as I struggled simultaneously to comprehend and to remain uninformed. "Are you saying that Dennis ran over another cat?"

"Bumped her with the car. The gray one, he stepped on. And one, I think, he lost — but that doesn't count, that happens. You didn't know that?"

"No."

On her cardboard slab, poor Icarus was stiffening fast. Mona watched me awhile. I was crying; I had been, I guess, all along. Finally she asked, "Did you know his first wife, by any chance?"

"Dennis's ex-wife? I haven't met her yet."

She laughed. "It's a little late."

"I would've met her when she dropped Raleigh off, but she was in a hurry."

"No, Raleigh's owner was Laura Lee, Dennis's third wife — they were only married a couple of months. I'm talking about his first one."

"What are you saying? That Dennis had another two wives?"

"Uh-oh," Mona said.

"Are you saying *I am Dennis's fourth wife?*"

"I think I'm out of line here."

"Wait! Tell me!" And, ashamed: "I didn't know about this."

"He should tell you."

"No. *You* should tell me. Please."

There was a long and busy silence. She studied the table and Icarus upon it, furry, twisted, and undeniably — it didn't take a licensed veterinarian to identify the problem — deceased. Mona said, "This is crazy. You really want to hear this?"

"I really do. I really, really do."

"Okay, but I don't think —"

"You tell me!" I grabbed her arm and gave it a vicious twist.

"Let go of me. Fine — it's up to you. Before Laura Lee, he had two earlier wives."

"And they got divorced?"

"One tried."

"One *'tried'?* And what happened?" My skin jumped. "What happened to the wives?" But inevitably, and much too slowly, it was becoming clear to me, like a gray dawn languidly breaking, that, as so often in matters involving my husband, I was not going to be happy to hear the news.

"One ran away," she said. "They never found her. She just — it was a remarkable thing. One day she just completely disappeared. She was gone."

"Did they look for her?"

"Of course they looked. Dennis wouldn't give up. They looked for years."

"It's rare for somebody to just disappear."

"You bet," Mona said.

"Do you think something happened to her?"

"What's your guess?" she asked, with genuine curiosity.

Scared to death: "And the other wife? The one who tried to get the divorce?"

She eyed me.

"What happened to the other wife?"

"I kind of hate to tell you."

"Tell me."

"Even for me, this is a lot to tell somebody."

I took a pugilist's stance, assuming a classic posture subtly suggestive of my total willingness to whip her butt. "Mona. You tell me what happened to the other wife."

Mona, after a complicated pause, both ominous and tactful: "Fell out the window."

I was panting. A cat and a frog lost to the same variety of incredibly bad luck that had also bumped off other creatures!

I'll hold the line! I won't fill up the yard! We would not bury Icarus together, Dennis and I, alongside Bianca under her myrtle blanket. Heroic Icarus, whose instinctive cat-efforts to prolong her own life by secreting herself behind winter coats had failed so miserably and, now I knew, unavoidably. I left her body with Mona and, my tongue dripping like Raleigh's, rushed out into

Brooklyn. I ran, past Middle Eastern grocery stores, *tac-querias* and check-cashing places, every step bringing me closer to the appalling home I had colluded in establishing as the fourth wife of my incomparably dangerous first and only husband.

They were waiting for me. They stood in the doorway and watched me climb the steps. I looked at Raleigh for some creaturely support, and he smiled, of course, a dog's smile.

Late at night. Moon rising.

"Mona told me some things. I need to ask you about —"

"You know I've been divorced."

"But apparently you also —"

He tossed in the bed like an earthquake starting. The moon slid above the rooftops and cast its darkling light into our undulating room. Beneath the sheet, I began to tremble.

"Dennis? Mona told me that you also had —" Something silenced me, some glance, some scent.

26

Still welcoming me home, Dennis cooked us the soft-shell crabs he had promised, and at five in the morning I woke and vomited. The day passed while I threw up. I said one thing to him: "I need sleep." I slept and dreamed that Bianca and Icarus still lived and were slowly expiring of numberless human errors, the irreparable malfeasances caused by my ill will and cowardice. My hand hung off the bed and Raleigh licked it raw.

It was only food poisoning. Couldn't this happen to anybody, anywhere?

Now, gone from our minds were my cameras, his computer, Goffman the sociologist, movies, holidays, weather, the residual possibility that a real peopled world existed and that Dennis and I might enter it. We were locked in something together. Mona could've told us that, Icarus surely knew, all along.

Here's what happened one week later:

First, Dennis plunging out of the house, heading for the bagel place, leaving the dead bolt protruding so the door doesn't shut. Next, Raleigh nosing the door open and hustling, excited, down the front steps. By now Den is across the street, and he turns. I reconstruct this quiet beginning from what Den told me, shuddering and sobbing in my arms, in the living room that night near dawn, before, harking back to some earlier time we had shared a lifetime ago, we fell asleep on the floor.

Den on one side of the street. Raleigh on the other, looking this way and that.

Den waves and calls.

Raleigh, ambivalent, as if he and Den have a rushing river between them — and perhaps feeling unusually exposed without being leashed to a hysterically commanding master — hesitates.

Den checks for cars. "Okay, Raleigh boy! Come! Come! *Come! Don't stall, boy! Don't stall!*"

Still the dog temporizes; Raleigh often does — often did. But with Den's next exhortations, Raleigh is galvanized. He yelps and prances off the curb. A pickup filled with soda cans comes clinking around the corner. Shriek of brakes.

When I got outside, at first I couldn't see Dennis. I could see Raleigh. He lay just under the truck's bumper with a little magic space around him. He looked like a dead dog, but when I reached him I saw that his eyes were open and he was breathing. Den rushed from the bagel shop screaming, "Don't move him! Mona's coming!" His shirt was unbuttoned as if he'd been rending his garments, and moisture, sweat like tears, shone on his frantic face. He ran up, stamped on my foot (later it would swell), tore off the shirt, and balled it up, tenderly, under Raleigh's warm and staring head.

Moments like hours later, we were truly trapped, apart, living in the separate timeless universe of the accident. We were four: me, kneeling in water in the street; Den, shirtless, standing, crouching, standing, wringing his hands; Hector, the incredibly handsome young Cuban man who had been driving the pickup, inside the bagel shop; and Raleigh, lying on his side with his eyes open, beautifully, intelligently silent, like somebody lost in wonderment.

There was room for cars to squeeze past us, and now they started doing it, pausing, gliding on. Hector emerged from the bagel place where he'd been phoning his mother, his brother, his sisters, and his wife. He had people to call! — people whose love and counsel sustained him in terrible moments, people who, in some genuinely crucial way, could help. Dennis and I had only Mona.

Raleigh looked at me. I held his paw. I ran my fingers over the tough pads, the silky strips of fur between them. I set my hand on his back and felt his quick heart beating.

As I say, Hector emerged. Walking around and around, circling the truck, he began pounding his gorgeous thighs. "I killed your dog," he said. "This is a terrible thing. A dog, for an American family, is a family member. Oh, how terrible. I was driving too rapidly for the situation! Why didn't I watch more carefully? The dog is dead and I am to blame."

You didn't do it, Hector. Somebody else did it.

Dennis said, "He's not dead, man."

Hector said, "Soon the dog will be dead. How can I find forgiveness for myself?"

"Not so fast, guy," Den said. "This dog is not dead."

Raleigh lay and gazed at me, as if serenely. Then, with a sort of whir like a motor starting, he began to tremble.

Hector stood over Raleigh and me and dealt himself a few crushing blows on the arm. "He is dying. He is a dead dog any minute."

I ignored Hector, with a sense of actively avoiding a lunatic.

"The dog is near the gates of death."

Dennis jumped up, dwarfing the guy. He cried, "This dog is still with us, man! You pronounce this dog dead one more fucking time and I'm gonna deck you!"

Hector backed up with a quick rumba step, only to press on. "The truth is visible," he said mildly. "I am sorry."

"You're riding for it, man!"

Dennis was quite correct. Hector, I suppose, was now either entirely in the grip of a self-destructive compulsion or simply insanely heedless of potential danger to himself; or — thinking about it in a related way — in what could not yet be called the aftermath of anything, he was already vigorously seeking punishment and some consequent absolution. I told him, "It might be better to not talk for a few minutes." I stroked Raleigh's hot silky head.

Hector murmured, "I think the dog is just about dead."

Den screamed, *"Shut the fuck up! You better hope this dog ain't dead, man, because if this dog is dead I'm gonna fucking put out your lights!"*

Hector whispered, "Say good-bye to your beautiful furry dog," and Dennis sprang at him and tried to punch him in the nose. Hector jumped out of reach. Den grabbed him and got Hector's head clamped under one arm; Hector struggled and kicked his feet. Den pressed Hector's cheek against his bare chest and smacked him in the head, shrieking, *"You gonna shut your fucking face the fuck up?"*

Meanwhile, Raleigh looked at me, closed his eyes, and died.

Oh, Raleigh. Oh, sweetheart.

I saw him go. Raleigh's fundamental self in invisible but discernible form lifted from his body and rose in the air, past the place where Dennis and Hector were disconsolately scuffling, past some observers gathering on the sidewalk, past the bagel sign up near the roof. Raleigh's spirit, always so capacious, expanded as it rose. It was a rectangular shape with rounded corners, larger than his body; behind it, the colors of the bagel shop and Hector's truck and the rest of the concrete world turned slightly fainter as it passed. This transparent shape, the shape of his future coffin and full of

Raleigh's eager sweetness, ascended fast and, as it reached the height of a second story, dispersed into ordinary air. And our gentle, deranged, mysterious, irreplaceable dog-friend was gone.

Mona's van pulled up. Den released his grip on Hector and let him drop. Raleigh's fur began to cool under my hand. Hector was the first to start to cry.

This was a moment we had been waiting for. It was strangely but unmistakably akin to that instant, after the wedding ceremony and the dancing and the cake-feeding and the toasts, when a door shuts behind the bridal couple and they are finally and for the first time alone: Their marriage begins. For Dennis and me, that door closed now, that moment came. Together, always.

In the days after Raleigh's death, life was without savor. We couldn't eat, we couldn't sleep, we couldn't bear to speak to each other or to be apart. Without our Raleigh boy, in some true sense there was no point in going on. I could smell the dog with me all the time. I could smell fresh turds, though there couldn't be any, now, in the garden — an olfactory hallucination, a phantom odor like the feel of a "phantom limb."

As Raleigh himself had once seemed the canine incarnation of Den's overexuberance, now Dennis began to grow doggier every day. He turned in a circle before taking a seat; he stepped into the garden to pee against trees; he wandered from room to room staring mutely out of wet canine-like eyes. In the night I pressed my rump against his and he was trembling like a pup.

After three days, he finally said, "I'm the one who made him cross the street. I killed my dog."

There was, of course, only one true response to this: Yes, you did. I said, "Don't think that way."

"I killed him." Just like Hector. "Oh. My dog is dead and it's my fault."

"It was a mistake."

"It was me."

Craftily, I said, "It was not intentional, it was a terrible accident. You're mourning him and you can't think straight and of course you feel at fault — I feel *I'm* at fault. Don't abuse yourself."

But, *entre nous:* Bianca, Icarus, and Raleigh. It was getting crowded in pet heaven.

I knew, Den did kill them.

I'll be next.

27

Now quiet courtesy was my watchword. His, too. The summery air of Brooklyn smelled faintly of wood smoke. The leaves of our maple would soon turn and fade; when they had fallen, I'd be gone.

As I sat in the garden in late August sunlight, pretending to scrutinize contact sheets and trying to plan, Dennis walked behind me and set his hands on my shoulders, and I shuddered.

Secretly, I was packing. Secretly, he knew. He murmured, into my hair, apropos nothing: "I've been left before."

"I know, Den. I apologized."

"I don't mean you. I mean somebody else. Somebody left me a long time ago."

"Who?"

"It doesn't matter."

I stopped him. I said that I'd been waiting for a sensible moment to raise some important questions, that Mona had told me disturbing things, that it appeared that for whatever reason and perhaps even understandably he had not been entirely straightforward with me, and that in any case for a long time I'd been thinking in terms of a possible trial separation, and that I increasingly felt that things between us were —

"Not gonna happen," he said.

"Pardon me?"

He released my shoulders, stumbled, righted himself. He came around and stood in front of me. Breathless, he said, "I want to tell you."

"What is it?"

"Don't take this wrongly."

I looked at him. His nose was running, his hair awry. He looked flushed and hectic and cute and crazed.

"Can I tell you?"

I looked at him.

"I just want to say that I . . . can't let you leave."

I looked at him.

"I know I said that before, and I'm sorry about that, but this time it's true. I know I cried wolf."

I looked.

"Crying wolf was a big big mistake. Are you listening?"

"Of course."

"Please, I hope you'll pay attention to me now: Don't try to leave. Don't try to leave me. Do not try it. I cannot let it happen."

"At this point," I said, or murmured, "I'm just asking some questions, and I think we can plan together to —"

"No separation," he said.

"Well, I think we could —"

"Not gonna happen. No separations and no divorces. I've been divorced. It will never happen again. Are you telling me that you want to leave me?"

"I'm saying that you and I need to —"

"Are you leaving?"

"Well, right now I'm —"

"Are you thinking about leaving?"

"Den, I'm not really going anywhere, I'm just —"

"Good. That's good." And he turned and, thoroughly gracefully, quit the yard. Later, encountering me in the kitchen, he sidled up and massaged my shoulders, frightening me on behalf of my collarbone and its fragility and nearness to those vigorous fingers. He said again, with creepy, fervent approval: "Good. Good."

This was a Tuesday, the end of August.

On Wednesday the toilet overflowed.

We couldn't fix it, and at last a plumber arrived, a portly, calm, thoughtful plumber. After he'd been in the bathroom awhile, I knocked. I wanted to stand next to him.

"Ma'am, don't come in."

"I need to take a look at something."

"It's not a great idea right now."

"Why not?" Only a few syllables into our discussion,

I was unmistakably drawing comfort from talking to the plumber through the door. I leaned forward and sniffed the wood.

"It's not pleasant in here right now. It's a little bit —"

I went in. The plumber was standing mystified in smelly water, on the cell phone to his boss. They could not figure it out. The plumber maneuvered his snake down the toilet to show me: snake met no obstruction. Then flushed to show me: toilet still overflowed. Me all eyes, all ears. Uh-huh, uh-huh. He said he had never encountered anything like this in thirty years, and my head wobbled like an infant's. "What could it be?" I asked. I was thinking dead animal. Of course these days I was thinking dead animal with regularity.

The decent plumber went to work, lifted off the whole toilet, and called me back to look into the base, right under the wax ring. We stood side by side, he and I, one astounded, one very frightened. We were gazing at a loaf of French bread.

"It's surprising," he said. "Your child must've dropped it in and flushed."

I was terrified. "We don't have children."

He stared at me, and I thought, *Let me go with you. Hide me in your closet.*

Downstairs, I watched over the plumber's solid shoulder while he wrote his notes describing the situation. He was obviously a natural problem solver. I liked his sturdy handwriting. Concentrating on his paperwork, he looked so sweet. I had the strong feeling that if I continued to show him the true interest I was developing in plumbing, he and I could become friends. "Why didn't you write what caused the stoppage?"

He said that would've been unprofessional. "Y'know how your lawyer's got to preserve confidentiality?"

"Yes?"

"Your plumber should do the same."

Then the plumber was gone. He had plumbed to good effect. We had had a mysterious stoppage and he had discreetly accomplished a remedy. I stood in the hallway remembering the plumber the way you'd recall a lover gone to war. Then Dennis burst out of the kitchen to deny that he had flushed the baguette.

On Thursday he totaled the car. Turned onto Montague Street against the light. He stepped out and walked home.

On Friday, nothing. Ominous nothing. Lowering skies and thunder without rain. We pretended calm.

On Saturday, he broke my arm.

The day began at eight, when I woke with a grim fearfulness, without the faintest idea where I was, or who. I rolled over and clicked through thirty channels, stopping at *Adam Smith's Money World*. Beside me Dennis woke, struggled up among the pillows, and stared at the TV, following closely as Adam prised some economic prognostications out of a meticulously shaved man in an elegant suit.

"Hi," I said, as if casually, startling Dennis, who moved in for a good-morning hug and, impossible though it may seem for someone to manage this while simultaneously resting in bed, lurched. "Oh, don't!" But he crookedly dropped his entire weight, his heat, his zeal, all his Dennisness, on my left forearm, and it cracked.

Pain genuinely blinding; sound truly sickening, like a pencil snapping; and, really, no surprise. Noticing Den's chagrin, hearing Adam Smith expressing his groundless confidence that we viewers could truly comprehend money and its world and bidding us good-bye for now, fighting for consciousness, I passed out.

The ride was as always, perilous and long. By agreement, though silently (since I was just emerged and incompletely from my sudden nap), we propped me in the van (since, as I say, he had destroyed the Alfa earlier in the week) and drove into Manhattan to Beth Israel Hospital (since we had "used up" — Den's formulation — all the Brooklyn emergency rooms, which is to say we'd brought them so many accidents, or "accidents," that the computer would surely red-flag the guy and remand him to prison on the spot). The usual triage and tedium and pain and fear, the setting of the bone, the familiar descent into Percocet twilight. Much later, I lay — we three lay — diagonally across our scarifying bed: me, my plaster cast, and Dennis mournfully nipping at his grubby fingernails.

Why not leave? Even now. Hobbled or whole, people do it. Go at night.

Reclining there with my snapped arm, I rehearsed my earlier, failed departures and saw that they had occurred in a moment never to return. I took time to imagine one final, true leave-taking, and the more I conjured it, the more the image lost color — it faded to sepia and wavered and then it was gone. First, I had nowhere near the resources it would take to pull off an escape. Even if a helicopter dropped into the prison yard to lift me away, what then? There wasn't enough cash in the borough of Brooklyn, including Brooklyn Heights, to shield me, should I attempt a run for it, from harm. I didn't possess anything like the big money I'd need to flee in the dark with my arm in a cast; fly to, say, Guadalajara or France; hire an army of bodyguards; buy false papers and plastic surgery and a correct wardrobe and a new profession; establish a fresh identity completely different from my recent and current one as the photographer-wife of a genuinely well-intentioned but finally lethal man; and live on. Dennis and I were in agreement: He would find me.

I couldn't see the clock — was the clock gone? "What time is it?"

"You've got time," he said, meaning what? Time for what?

On the Sunday before Labor Day, he gave me a concussion. Never mind how. A violent blow to a soft structure. It felt exactly like what it is.

28

I got a tic in my eye. I'd hold my head still, as the concussion victim must, and feel my eyelid, regular as a metronome, twitching with fear.

Tense watching, stealthy waiting.

On the following Wednesday, at last Dennis left his study and went out.

I limped to the computer. We've already established that another woman might've gotten herself to the car, to the lawyer. Two of my predecessors, of course, in what I could now only imagine must've been similar situations, had done those very things, and their efforts had proved not merely fruitless but disastrous, and those women's stories were cautionary in the extreme, having ended, as they did, so remarkably badly. Either I was much better informed than they or my aspirations were simply more modest: I wanted to get out alive.

I propped my arm in its cast on the desk. The fish quit swimming and the encyclopedia popped into view. Under "Poisons" were 277 entries. Soon I was slipping into a state of mingled hyperalertness and serenity; then followed the slowest, quietest hour I had spent in years. Time fell away as I consulted the computer's busy face, which was full of complicated ideas about how I could save my life.

First, the most famous strangulators, curare and hemlock. Then the time-honored ones with the beautiful evocative names, arsenic and belladonna, opium and chloroform, euphorbia and dumbcane. Two hundred kinds of poisonous mushrooms — satan's mushroom, jack-o'-lantern, death angel, and 197 more. Within moments I was pointing and clicking in an authentic trance, systematically considering with equal seriousness each potentially fatal option, from the actually possible to the probably unworkable to the patently absurd. There was calcium oxalate, for example, which is found in uncooked taro; I saw myself already anticipatorily arrayed in widow's black, in the steamy kitchen of the China Pearl dim sum restaurant, smelling some fishy garbage, glancing furtively at the prep cooks, slipping a blob of raw taro into a maroon polyester napkin. Or is fried taro actually taro *root*, and does that also carry the poison? I clicked onward.

Botulism kills, of course, but how do you make it happen — skulk to the supermarket and look for swollen cans?

Scorpions, pit vipers, death adders, copperheads, jellies. Gila monsters and beaded lizards and centipedes.
Asps! Where would I acquire one of these, and how to
handle it so as to avoid death to myself while accomplishing my goal? You can't just swaddle a jellyfish in a
towel and carry it into the living room and press it onto
your husband's chest.

The computer and I stepped into a magic garden,
where we encountered elderberry; you could die if you
playfully used an elderberry stem as a blowgun or straw.
But this could hardly plausibly be introduced into Den's
and my exchanges, neither of us being, these days, in a
sportive mood. Same problem with wisteria; I'd have to
stroll around the garden with Den and lightheartedly
persuade him to eat a large number of seeds or pods.

Baneberry. Causes severe gastroenteritis if eaten,
but — damn! — "rarely with fatal results." With Den's
and my luck, he'd chow down, shit all over the rugs, and
bounce back to vibrant life.

Autumn crocus. No good. Native to Europe.

Bracken destroys bone marrow. But wouldn't that take
years? Same flaw with the heavy metals, lead and mercury.

Star-of-Bethlehem looked and sounded wonderful,
with its erect linear leaves and white clusters of blossoms: "The bulbs, which may be brought to the surface
by plowing or by frost heaving, contain poisons." Oh, I
loved this — the arrival of cold nights, the inexorable
rising of the bulbs through layers of frozen soil and
loam, the accidental ingestion of the onionlike spheres,

and then the amazing triad of predeath symptoms experienced by the unlucky sufferer whose last act on earth was to mistake deadly plant material for lunch: *depression, salivation,* and *bloat.*

And, more generally, what a revelation: that in some crucial sense Den and I, the most preternaturally sequestered couple imaginable, were not alone. That the perilous world of our shared home was actually microcosmic: The known universe comprises the noxious and toxic! What is it that prevents people, any day of the week, from idly nibbling a few sprigs of lily of the valley and going into a decline? Horseshoe crabs, daphne bushes, climbing bittersweet, red tide — how do any of us survive at all? So many things could kill with dispatch, and all of them called to me.

I couldn't make out from its description whether mistletoe is a poison or an antidote. Wasn't that apt?

Cyanide derives from wild cherries!

Yews cause heart block! Let's say you ingest some yew foliage — and the matter of how you would reach the point of chewing and swallowing yew needles stirred in me an intense and preoccupying curiosity — anyway, eat them and your inevitable decline would be the biochemical equivalent of crashing into a wall. Your heart would stop so suddenly that no symptoms would appear. You would simply drop dead.

Ingest some locoweed and you'll spend your last days experiencing hallucinations, a slow gait, and lusterless hair.

Ingest some buckeye horse-chestnuts and paralysis is certain.

Ingest some amanitas and you're bound for an elegant descent: jaundice, cyanosis, coma, and death.

Ingest a fly mushroom, with its yellow cap and white gills and the soft torn frill of its —

The door slammed.

He was back.

I exited with rapid-fire clicks and flew downstairs as if pursued.

Both shuddering, we embraced.

Now of course I could not sleep. Midnight came and went, night slid across the ceiling, sunrise deepened into morning, while I waited and watched, my heart flopping in my chest. Eyelid atwitter, I lay next to dreaming Dennis, panting as if in flight.

Sometimes, we know, an idea will take a very long time coming to consciousness. It will rise to just under the mind's surface and lie there for months, even years. At last, bringing relief and a sense of inevitability and of simple correctness almost disorienting in its clarity, it'll pop through.

Strychnine.

*

I went to find rat poison.

Carrying my bashed head tenderly, favoring my atrophying arm in its plaster cast, shivering, in depressing fluorescence in a vast twenty-four-hour drugstore in Queens I cruised the aisles.

In the fishing supplies department, soon I stood hefting lead weights — four-pound balls, eight-ounce silver torpedoes, tiny river sinkers. A red sign warned me that after handling these products, as I was extensively doing, I must not put my hands into my mouth because the product contained lead, known by the State of New York to cause birth defects or reproductive harm. My first thought: Too late, he's already born.

I ranged farther afield. Down the aisle were displayed fascinating tools, steelhead spinners for trout, worm threaders and squid jigs — my mind entertaining itself with the interesting notion that I didn't intend to kill him, only to catch him. Into my basket I set a useless but, I thought, emblematic six-pack of size-four Eagle Claw snelled fishhooks, whose slogan was "They hook and hold." Like Dennis himself; he hooked and held. Like me now, clinging to something whose outlines I could not see. "Excuse me," a man muttered, and I jumped a foot. My eyelid twitched wildly. But he only wanted to compare rods.

Why temporize further, loitering in fishing gear? While somebody needed to be permanently stopped in his tracks. I stepped — not casually but urgently, for any interested drug-supermarket patron to observe — into the pest-extermination aisle.

Strychnine causes, to its consumer, "extreme excita-
tion of the central nervous system." This seemed so fit-
ting, allusive as it was to the ordinary condition of my
Dennis at rest. The rat poison here, however, didn't
appear dependably lethal; it contained neither the afore-
mentioned strychnine nor thallium sulfate, both excellent substances with which I was now conversant.
Would these pellets, then, really kill the rat? According
to the box, the poison's flavor was tasty to a rodent and
his extermination could be accomplished in one feeding; then the fine print admitted the rat would not actually breathe his last for four to five days! I chuckled
bitterly — such a delay would be unacceptable — and
when a woman in a babushka looked at me, with my
good hand I shot her the bird.

Additionally, the box asserted, accurately I'm sure, it
was a violation of federal law to use the rat-killing product
in a manner inconsistent with its labeling, that is to deploy
it for the elimination of any creature other than a rodent.
Who cared! Toxicological crime detection was nothing to
me now. Let the bozos tail me, let 'em dust for my prints!
Lost in Queens with my brain ringing and my arm in a
sling, growing monstrous, laughing a monster laugh.

I am not the problem. He is the problem and see what I
have become. Solipsism doesn't kill or we would've long
since been a pair of dead ducks.

Anyway Dennis and I were reaching the end of our
solitary road.

Farther down the street, in a hardware store, I considered some Deadline: One Last Meal for Slugs and Snails. I considered —

Whoa! Pay dirt! Quick Action Gopher Mix. Here it was: 99.5 percent inert ingredients, to be sure, but also one-half of one percent strychnine! With a long-handled spoon, maybe a silver Danish iced-tea spoon like the one I had used to stir my beloved killer's sugar into his tea (the cloud of tiny grains swirling in the glass preparatory to being absorbed — I stood recalling that little sugar cloud with a jolt of sudden sexual passion, which, after long and tiresome effort, I managed to get tamped down in the service of regaining focus and continuing my important shopping trip) — with a spoon you'd insert one teaspoon of poison into the main runway system of the burrowing gopher's underground tunnels, and the gopher would literally bite the dust.

This could be done. (Extrapolate from a gopher to a man.) I stumbled to the counter. It was too dark in here. My tic was going wild. I glanced around in the gloom with febrile eyes, whose pupils, I knew, were dilated to a truly attractive black like those (again I knew from my lavish poison research) of a sixteenth-century Italian courtesan on belladonna. I told the clerk, who manifestly didn't give a shit, "I need to try this stuff. But we might not actually have gophers."

The clerk reached out, I thought to touch my broken arm.

"Get back!"

"Whaddaya mean, 'get back'? I'm nowhere near you," he said, bagging my purchase.

"Just don't touch me!"

"Not on a bet, lady," and our transaction drew to a close.

Exiting with my package, I didn't bear a grudge. With wonderful economy of gesture he had rung up my gopher-murder powder. Although the hardware store man and I had got off on the wrong foot and didn't like each other and would never change our minds, out on the sidewalk I already recalled him fondly. I had been delighted by his manual dexterity, all that small motor coordination so beautifully, so simply deployed. I had watched him make change with a turbulent fascination almost like lust. In that dusky store I had stood entranced, a voyeur of everyday gracefulness.

Wanted a gun but didn't know exactly how to get one.

Two doors down, bought a big wide hunting knife in a leather sheath.

Bought rope. What for? You never know! Keep those options wide open.

Through the bright September day, by expensive taxicab, one last time I traveled home. I plunged up the steps, hobbling and weaving, crippled in more ways than I could elucidate yet undeniably better armed than I had ever been in my life.

Stowed my purchases under the claw-foot bathtub.

Beneath the duvet swarming with invisible allergenic dust mites and their waste products, I fell unconscious for the first time in days and slept off my adrenaline binge.

29

I woke suddenly, of course afraid.

I could hear him in the house.

I thought he was pawing something, like our late dog.

My toe throbbed where he'd broken it months ago, my neck ached where he'd wrenched it, my forearm, needless to report, itched in its plaster cast. My head, as you know, was concussed, and my ears rang.

Now Den came in, bounced off the doorjamb, and, scattering the four hundred yellow pages of his first draft everywhere around him, crashed to the rug. I gazed at him as though from far away. He muttered, "Don't look like that."

"I didn't look like anything."

"You ridiculed me."

"I didn't intend to." Though perhaps I had. Who knows anymore?

"You had a ridiculing look."

"Oh," I whispered, "Dennie."

Much later — it is always much later, you've noticed, in our story — when night came, I wrestled myself out of bed and started for the bathroom. As Raleigh once had, Den scrambled up and followed and waited outside the door. When finally I reemerged, Dennis, reaching to help me, knocked me down. I fell, twisting my body to hold my cast in the air; he trod on my right knee; he cried, *"Oh my god! I'm sorry! Honey!"* And together we escorted me back to bed, he helping me, I protecting me from his help.

I am going to kill my husband.

I was tremulous, as people will be after a narrow escape: He had not crushed my patella. However, though we elevated and iced, within an hour a giant's hematoma had blossomed below my right knee. Me dreaming and waking. Dennis everywhere, here and there, my whole world.

I am going to kill my husband. We tried to sleep.

All night he lay near me, worrying aloud and calling to me as from another country while I dozed and woke. By dawn the leg had become an immense columnar thing. It didn't seem to be attached to me. I was shuddering and too cold. I opened my eyes. With tears in his, he stood over me. "Hospital," he said.

"No." He would, for sure, approach the emergency room, peel into the lot, and plow the van into a wall. In

fact they couldn't even pretend to help anymore, the
emergency room personnel of several boroughs. All of
them knew us. None had saved us. I would take my
chances here at home, where this began. "No hospital.
I'll be okay."

"Sweetheart, I'm so sorry."

"I'm okay." Though I wasn't, cold with shock and
steadily rising fear. I was decidedly not okay, with my
hematoma, ringing head, plaster cast, arthritic toe, bad
memories, twisted character, deadly plans.

Too late for poison.

While I feigned dreamless sleep, the future dead man
wrote a long and inclusive grocery list, as for a bomb
shelter. Recumbent and waiting, gazing at blackness
inside my eyes, I was also kind of — how shall I say
it? — getting a kick out of this moment: blameless Dennis making jolly plans for major provisioning as though
our once abundant life together were going to endure,
chock-full of the quotidian, nice and lasting and normal.
Dennis was a deluded, happy man, gazing at the light
from a dead star. In the morning, after he tiptoed out to
buy his groceries, I rose with difficulty from our marriage bed, to visit our home for what I suddenly knew
might be the last time.

I thought for a moment to descend to the basement to
say good-bye to Bianca, but, as you know so well, she
was gone. On my sequoia-trunk leg I clumped downstairs and out into the garden to shed a last tear on the

myrtle surmounting her little frog's grave. Back inside, I eased myself from room to room, the deformed leg dragging, the foot starting to drop alarmingly, but why worry now? I was saying farewell. In remembrance of brave Icarus, whose cat-resourcefulness had so inspiringly prolonged her doomed life, I opened the closet, observed the coats on their hangers, touched their woolen sleeves. I spent a long time prostrate on the pumpkin-colored chaise longue, nose to the velvet, breathing some last pungent sniffs of the residual scent of — oh, our best boy! — Raleigh.

Then I hobbled up.

Third-floor bathroom. It took a long time to get there. But I had time.

30

What if I had truly run for it, with the killer for my boyfriend, with the frog, or alone? Just stayed on the highway.

Now, waiting in the bathroom at the top of the stairs, I saw the story of the road unfolding. I saw Dennis back at the house, preparing to follow — all the lamps ablaze, the brownstone like a dressed ship, and Dennis running through the bright rooms. Den finding his mud-caked shoes, locating his keys, stuffing clothes into bags, hurling the bags out the door. The van waiting, doors open, motor ticking. Den furious, focused, slipping and sliding, his eye on the ball. Soon he'll be tailing me, driving too.

In this fantasy, I drive for half a year.

Winter comes.

Ice fogging the windshield. In the night, a subfreezing night with high winds, I'm following a black highway under a string of lights, the Alfa shuddering in the gusts. I round a curve, and, ahead, far over in the right lane, is a small glowing lavender oblong — something not yet recognizable but utterly familiar. Glow of neon outlining a license plate. Exactly like, I think slowly, the neon frame — like mine. The one he gave me. I'm almost upon it, plunging past in the dark, and I see the shape of the slow-moving vehicle attached to the luminous floating rectangle enclosing the plate with its known numbers. My van. I pass. In the mirror, black night falling off, and my pursuer picking up speed.

Of course no van in the world can overtake an Alfa Romeo. I can outrun him, and drive months more, and, in the spring, descend. In May I'll drop from Vermont, still in winter with infinitesimal red buds of maples, down into forsythia and pear blossoms and greenness, into fragrant winds, under a lowering sky. At Port Chester, the trees will be chartreuse and the sun pouring brilliance all over them; in New Jersey, velvet lawns and everything in full leaf; in North Carolina, the dead center of long true springtime; in Charleston, tropical heat, steam hanging over the blue harbor. I will drive on.

Instead, I slow, after half a year of flight, and pull off the road to wait for him in the cold and dark. And he —

The front door slammed.

Eye twitching, heart leaping. Breath coming fast.

"Honey?"

"I'm upstairs!"

"I'll be up! I've just gotta —! I bought you —! All this great stuff, I'll just —!" Then he rushed back and forth down there for a long time.

I could wait.

Tidily arrayed in my bathtub on pearly curving porcelain, my weapons reposed. While guileless Dennis, below, began his ascent, with my good hand I hefted my tools.

"Sweetheart?"

"I'm on the third floor!"

How had we two arrived so suddenly, so inexorably, at the moment when I secreted myself inside this white room with its view of the leafy crowns of trees growing in Brooklyn, and sat upon a wicker chair to await my husband's final entrance? This moment when I sat to wait with the objects that had become my everything, my claw-foot tub and my cameras, my knife, my rope. No blunt instrument, I realized too late — Colonel Mustard would've stockpiled a candlestick.

"Honey?"

"I'm on the third floor!"

"Where?"

"Bathroom!"

Mounting the first set of stairs, of course he tripped and dropped to one knee. I heard it, saw it. No problem. He'd right himself. Matter of time. Knife unsheathed, camera loaded, I heaved myself to a standing position and got braced against the edge of the tub.

"Sweetheart?"

"I'm in the bathroom!"

"Where are you?"

"Upstairs bathroom!"

"Where are you?"

"Up here!"

"In the tub?" Innocent Dennis inside his own home, clambering upward, blind to the future in which his novel will remain forever unfinished, his former pets will lie forever underground, his flawed but immutable marriage will turn out to have lasted until the end of his life.

He will mount the lower stairs, pause at the landing sliding his hand along the banister's smoothness, walk the flowered carpet of the second-floor hallway, set his foot on the bottom step of the upper stairs, trip and recover, and finally, inevitably, calling to me all the while, ascend.

I'll be juggling everything like Wesley the boy juggler. That's my job — to make this come out right.

Leaning against the tub, I rehearsed: balance the Leica on my cast, shoot the flash, it blinds him some, knife behind my back, call out my apologies loud and true, and lunge. Blood, certainly, hideous, apt. We are counting on me for a denouement as unimaginable as it will be correct. Then I'll sit on the cool tile floor of the white red-splattered bathroom and I'll hold his hand and we'll rest awhile.

*

My darling, my victim, he will climb, knock, open the door. I'll see his face; he'll see mine. Lift the camera, blind him, two steps forward, clump clump, raise the knife. How can I do it? But I must, for both of us. And, of course, he's Dennis; he'll help me: He'll present his chest. He'll present his heart.

31

And after all that — well, how to break the impossible news? Dennis didn't arrive.

Instead, a telephone rang, so distant, so mundane, and somewhere halfway through his climb he answered it.

Who called that day I will never know. What reckless individual, after all, would have thought to contact either of us, this late in the game? To restate the obvious, our former friends and acquaintances had long since identified Den and me as a big fat wrong number.

After the call — maybe that's when he put on his new blue socks, just a simple pair of socks unfamiliar to me. A toilet flushed. He descended to the first floor. Then I could hear him in the foyer, and then — what a surprise! — the front door clicked behind him, and the house fell still. Dennis had gone out.

If events ever unfolded precisely as human beings expected, our lives would be even more astounding than

they are. As my epinephrine level dropped, I was too
shaky to continue leaning against the tub, so I pivoted
on my good leg and took a seat. The wicker creaked as
I settled myself anew and, in a convalescent fashion,
glanced experimentally around the bathroom.

Wow. Was this guy born under a lucky star, or what?
In short, the moment had passed.

Timing is everything. When a moment is gone, it's just
gone.

I sat there a long time — I can't, now, remember how
many hours, but I know night fell. When the sky was
black and Den hadn't returned, I heaved myself up and,
departing that lavatory brightness, hobbled down
through the house to store the clothesline alongside the
gopher poison in the basement where it belonged. The
dark cave of the basement, now as lifeless as once, during the tenure of darling Bianca, it had been vital — how
brutally the place had been transformed into a container
for abandoned tools! I felt my way down the steps, into
damp still air. After the white blaze of the bathroom, my
pupils were shrunk to pinpoints — I was pretty much
blind. I could feel the darkness purring around me. The
Leica, hanging by its strap around my neck, bumped my
chest as I groped my way. I was gripping, in my good
hand, the hunting knife, now sheathed, and clumping
around in the interior dusk like a fucked-up hunter. I
was scrabbling for a hiding place — if Dennis should
discover the obviously newly purchased weapon, how

could I explain? It occurred to me I might gift-wrap it and position it centrally on the hall table sporting a big acetate bow. Or maybe this didn't scan. If only we had a woodsman friend! I made my way into a corner and, with a humorous stabbing motion, tucked the knife behind a stack of logs.

At which point a floorboard, above, classically, creaked.

"Dennis?"

Creak.

"Dennis?"

Another creak, up there inside our house.

"Den?"

There was silence. I limped through the shadows and stood on the little scrap of Persian rug at the foot of the stairs (Bianca's rug, as we had thought of it — now, of course, Bianca's memorial rug). *"Den?"* Muffled footfalls and no answer. My pupils were widening but not fast enough. My camera nestled against my heart, and my heart started pumping too fast. Inside my chest, a crazed animal hurled itself against the bars of its cage. *"Den? Is that you?"*

Above me, the basement door slowly cracked. I couldn't see it but I heard it. "Dennie?" All the hairs standing up on my arms and my chest thudding. I could feel him above. I looked up.

I saw his socks.

It was so terrifying in that moment, the blue, unfamiliar footwear. Two feet were standing there in the socks, standing carefully, silently, on the top step, and when I called — as though casually, but pleading too — there was no reply.

"Den?" — my voice not immediately recognizable to my own ear, husky with fear now, all this fear rising like water and starting to spill — "Den? Is it you?"

At last, my husband's voice dropped down to me from somewhere up there, pronouncing four sinister words: "I've got a surprise."

And then the feet in their socks slid almost lazily from under him, the cuffs of his trousers came into view, and his legs flipped up. Dennis was falling. His body torqued, and his arms flew out, and, literally headfirst, he plummeted toward where I stood shuddering, holding my camera at the ready, poised to photograph — what? What life would bring. Dennis was plunging through strange cloudy air, and time slowed, and I took a single step in his direction before, in a sudden hurry, he smashed to the concrete floor in the dark at the bottom of our house.

We were entwined. Basement dust filled my nostrils. He had knocked me down, bounced a little, and passed out. From half underneath him, I peeked at his placid face — he was lying so unnaturally still, one arm folded across his chest and his eyes softly closed.

His hand lay curled around what was too obviously my surprise package, an innocent ring box, crimson velvet with a hinged lid, now sprung open. I twisted my neck to peer into the tiny blood red world, to see what was glittering there. It was a ring bearing a worked gold lily pad, and upon this shining leaf crouched a tiny creature of pavé diamonds with emerald eyes alight. A frog.

But what was I doing, gazing at jewelry while there was a rescue to be made? And just then a spout of blood opened on the side of Dennis's head and started dripping into his ear.

My legs were hopping with fear. I shifted my cast out of my own way, shoved myself from under him, and prepared to struggle to my feet.

While I was thus engaged, my husband opened his glimmering eyes.

"Den, can you talk?"

He could talk! He whispered: "Stay with me."

"Oh, Dennie, I'm so glad you woke up!"

He gripped my hand — even reclining there in gruesome disarray, he was still somewhat strong. He spoke too quietly, almost whimpering, with a sort of ravaged, insistent gentleness. "Don't go."

"You hit your head. Your head is bleeding. You passed out for a minute."

"It hurts too much," he whispered. "Please. It's too much for me."

"I'll call an ambulance."

But he held on. I could feel my metacarpal bones crunching together in his mitt. "Bend down," Dennis murmured, and I leaned close to his mouth. Tiny puffs of minty-smelling carbon dioxide, hot and short, against my ear; I was overwhelmed with tenderness for those urgent helpless little breaths. "You can stay with me the whole time," he whispered. "It's where you ought to be."

He was so sweet. He was the sweetest, all messy and sweaty and muddy and bloody, and I got amazing fresh bright-red head-wound blood just slathered all over me. "Sweetheart," he said, "I want you to stay with me. I want you to keep touching me. I need your help." Oh, his mournful and trusting gaze, as he whispered this old, old news.

In the halcyon past when our future had stretched before us, Dennis had often told me — dilating, I supposed, on Goffman — about leave-taking behavior. People on the point of parting suddenly converse; in the moments of farewell, they find their voices. Now, in the unthinkable present, I got down on my good elbow, and, strange to say, we spoke a short while. No accusations came from my direction; nor did my husband remark that the secret injuries I had caused him during our shared time had been manifold and irreparable, though how correct a statement that might have been. On the little rug, Dennis and I briefly, finally lay, accomplishing our last collusion, whispering together like the true companions we were.

While we talked, I saw something; but I didn't tell Dennis, not to alarm him. At the ground-level window, a flicker, a shadow, a fringe of whitish hair: Wesley! The little mournful juggler, I suddenly knew with certainty, had unaccountably selected this moment to step across the heretofore unbridgeable divide between his place and ours. I saw, or thought I saw, his silver earrings, and his liquid eyes wondering, before I took Dennis's hand in mine. Dead Goffman, I reminded myself, would have approved of this tie-sign, my unequivocal demonstration of Den's and my affinity; in Dennis's and my moment most extreme, I showed dear Wes at the window: I'm with him.

It was claustral here, and deeply quiet, at the foot of our basement stairs. Dennie passed out again. I shoved at his shoulder, but I couldn't rouse him. I pushed, and loudly called, but he would not wake. This terrible metallic blood smell. The hair on the side of his head was growing gluey and matted, but I was able to stroke his forehead, which was cool and damp, as though misted with evening dew. It seemed so dark, like a starless night. We seemed to be drifting through some bleak and shadowy sky. In a sudden access of the grief that will mark my life until the moment my own death arrives, I lay down again — one final time, with my face turned toward him, the concrete floor cold beneath my cheek — and I gazed at my husband where, paler and paler, supine on his scrap of blood-moistened rug, he was beginning to float away.

Sometime after Den's and my really quite brief chat together in the dark well of the basement, as things will in moments of trauma, things got scrambled. Eventually, I know, I told two detectives and a patrolman about the terror I had felt, an incapacitated woman alone in a cellar at night, hoping to save her unconscious husband who was bleeding way too profusely from a horrible freak-accident skull fracture.

Even before the police came to see me, I had already panted out our story to the no-nonsense but compassionate 911 guys, inside the rocketing ambulance, as they were using a bag to force oxygen into Dennis's lungs, while his heart rate dropped and his blood pressure rose and the siren shrieked around us.

By the time the police came and went, I had also already told everything to the senior resident at the hospital (an appealing guy, definitely harried and tousled, but what could be more understandable, given his obvious chronic sleep deprivation?). They immobilized Dennis on a backboard, although as I say he was already inert, and they fastened a cervical collar around his neck, and still he didn't wake up. They opened his eyelid, and my husband stared back at them as if alarmed, his pupil black and huge. They knew he was forty-two years old and they worked like dogs. They were preparing to drill a hole in his skull, when he died.

"In these cases, every second counts," the senior attending physician told me hours later, when I was still seated in a yellow plastic chair in the emergency-room lobby as though I were awaiting Den's imminent release to my care.

I looked at him, wondering. I was thinking, I blame the socks.

"With a blow like this to the side of the head, the

skull fracture tears the middle meningeal artery, and what you get is an arterial bleed to the brain," he said. "The skull is an enclosed space, normally just holding the brain and cerebrospinal fluid. When blood fills up the space, the skull can't expand." With rare candor, this physician, king of the ER, actually explained it all this way, in an undeniably sincere but completely inadequate attempt to answer my question How could this happen? "Do you understand?" he said. "So pretty soon the brain herniates down into the brain stem. And that's it."

Well, that's *not* it.

Dennis is not gone.

I do not accept it. Dennie will always be with me.

I'll need a support group! Of course my grief is indescribable and so I will not describe it — except to say those terrible words: I miss my husband. Still, I want to make contact with other widows who have lost men to electrical mishaps, Saturday afternoon falls from ladders, drownings in the tub. I want us to sit in a circle in comfy chairs, drinking decaffeinated beverages, recalling our darlings until we think we'll be able to sleep.

I'll show my new sisters his final photograph. In extremity, as legions can testify, people do extraordinary things. I didn't lift a sedan off Dennis. However, I did take his picture. While we waited for 911 to arrive, what the hell, the camera was loaded, it wasn't going to disturb an unconscious man, so I snapped a last shot. The dusty concrete floor. The rug. The blood. The flash illuminated like sudden lightning the sad dark basement in which we found ourselves, my husband and I, in some way I have to believe of one mind, at last together and so truly at home.

As I told Wesley Rolfe (when I got back from the hospital and there he was, wan but determined, waiting for me in the rapidly cooling September night on the stoop): This will take years.

I hate to keep going over it again and again. But that repetition is precisely what the staggered mind needs. As I pointed out, and as Wesley and the police detectives agreed without hesitation, I had been at an overwhelming disadvantage. How fast, realistically, could any woman have disentangled herself and regrouped and scrambled up a steep flight of shadowy stairs to a telephone, in the literally crippled condition in which almost innumerable earlier events had left me?

Of course I dialed 911! With trembling fingers! As any wife would!

Judge me if you can. I took my time.

The Dangerous Husband

A READING GROUP GUIDE

*The day I had scheduled for the death of my
husband dawned early and suddenly, with a
lucid blue sky.*

As ingenious as it is heartbreaking, *The Dangerous Husband*
is the story of a marriage that is not, after all, exactly like
everyone else's.

Or is it?

Jane Shapiro responds to readers' questions about *The Dangerous Husband*

How would you describe your own book?

As a dark—I suppose very dark—comedy about isolation, the American preoccupation with romantic love, above all the entanglements of marriage. As a sometimes desperately jolly, often vulgar, undeniably morbid tale about the longings and terrors, the erotic lives and lonelinesses and collusions of couples.

Your first novel, After Moondog, *was also the story of a marriage gone wrong. Recently one reviewer elegantly described you as "an uncommonly shrewd and discerning observer of the shifting tectonics of . . . marriage." What is it about the state of matrimony that inspires your creative spirit?*

It's been nearly twenty years since I've lived with a man, and in those years I've increasingly embellished my idea of the institution: Marriage, that mystery, seems fascinating. How the hell does it work? My own experience was of inhabiting a self-contained world—the partners collaborate in building the world and then, at least in contemporary America, they're alone in it together. And they're pretty much equally implicated in the result. *After Moondog* and *The Dangerous Husband* are so different—the first realistic and the second fantastic—but, for me, both books are about this complicated collaboration. And about how tenacious is marriage's hold on the partners—about the divorces that people can't quite finish.

I almost think of *After Moondog* and *The Dangerous Husband* as flanking the shelf of books I might've written about romantic love and loneliness and hapless individuals not unlike myself trying and failing to find wedded bliss—but never divorcing.

When you began writing, did you expect The Dangerous Husband *to be so dark?*

I didn't know what to expect. I set out. My friend Joyce Oates once commented about *After Moondog* that none of its characters could ever do anything really bad to each other, and I think now that I wanted to write an entirely different sort of sad and comic book about marriage, in which everybody does truly horrible things. As I worked on the book, it seemed to get blacker and funnier and so much odder than I had remotely anticipated.

The Dangerous Husband *has moments of great hilarity but also of great poignancy. Were there scenes that were hard to write? What was the greatest challenge you faced when writing this novel?*

For me, most scenes aren't hard to write—finding the voice of the book is hard. I wanted a narrator who thinks herself a reasonable being, who may even appear to be a victim, but who is finally at least as unhinged, and at least as lethal, as her husband. She reports the details of events with precision and in fact she's extremely unreliable—it becomes increasingly clear that we cannot trust her report. The challenge for me was in finding and maintaining her voice.

Where did the inspiration for the ill-fated pets come from?

In order for this story to work, my couple must be isolated in the world they've made together—their friends, their avenues of escape, must fall away. But a whole novel with only two important characters—it's kind of hard on the reader. So the sweet, lively, odd pets—and the house—are the other main characters.

In so many ways, Dennis is a kind and loving man, but his romantic gestures are often what make him a threat. Are his innocent bumblings a metaphor for other ways in which men threaten their marriages or the health of their wives?

If so, then the wife's moves may reflect the ways in which some women threaten their marriages. It's not at all the case here that the wife is a victim and the husband is a villain. She and he meet and fall in love and wed, and of course without noticing it they grow truly enmeshed; meanwhile his disorderliness, a sort of real derangement, increasingly reveals itself; the couple's home slowly becomes less the expected sanctuary than a life-threatening environment; to save herself, as she sees it, she'll have to sacrifice him: Finally the couple are pretty much equally dangerous to each other. The book could've been called *The Dangerous Couple*—it's more accurate, it's just not as good a title.

The husband is an unusual person, to say the least. How were you able to create such a singularly accident-prone character?

Well, you can create any character. I know I was out for dinner with my friend and former husband, a natty dresser and passionate diner, and as always, he splashed his Italian silk tie.

I know I wanted to think about what happens in a new union when the honeymoon ends and each lover faces a grim reality: The beloved is not what he or she seemed. Another, much less appealing, even repellent, beloved emerges! Then, somewhat later, as the innocent flaw appears magnified beyond endurance: *I could kill him.* Actually, as we know, this happens all the time.

Do you know anyone like Dennis?

How could I, really? As the story develops, Dennis's clumsiness—like so much else in the novel—becomes magnified to such a degree that it's surreal. But in another way, he's such a good guy, like many we've all known—exuberant, generous, buoyant, and he cares.

Have you ever had similar experiences in your personal relationships?

This novel develops to a point where nobody has had such experiences. Still, of course, it's an autobiographical book: It contains my intensity, loneliness, insistent humor, ordinary wish for love—and my sense of the unique creation of two people that a close relationship is, a shared, incomparable world.

Do men fear you now?

What a good question. One man I don't know well, with whom I had been enjoying a pleasant flirtation, seems to be avoiding me; after reading some of *The Dangerous Husband,*

he told a friend that he could never trust "a person like Jane."
I had so expected him to appreciate my book's sparkling wit
and the cadences of its sentences! The men who loved me still
do—they already knew what I'm like. They make nervous
jokes if, like Dennis, they spill something, but then so do I—I
identify with the husband in the book as well as the wife.

When did you realize The Dangerous Husband *was the perfect
title? Was it always your working title, or did you find it late in
the game?*

First the frog came to me. Then the title came to me. Then I
began. Much later, I wondered, Who would write such a book?

Jane Shapiro discusses some influences on *The Dangerous Husband*

There were three pieces of writing I loved as a child that, however inaccurately I remember them, influenced this book:

Balzac's novella *Passion in the Desert,* which I read when I was about ten, was a favorite story, about a man who shares a cave with a beautiful, beloved black leopard. It contains the idea—central, of course, to *The Dangerous Husband*—that the loved one is threatening to one's very life.

At around the same time, I was memorizing Rodgers and Hart lyrics. A favorite was one of the last songs Lorenz Hart wrote, "To Keep My Love Alive," which tells the story of a woman who serially kills her several husbands in order to maintain her good opinion of them—I thought this was incomparably witty.

Finally, months after *The Dangerous Husband* was published, I suddenly recognized that I had rewritten a Damon Runyon story of about two pages that I read at eight or nine. I think it's about a wife who goes to the store to buy some rat poison "to poison a big rat." At the time, this seemed to me just so brilliant I could hardly stand it.

And then, in modest homage to Nabokov, I wanted to write the road trip without destination of an inordinately odd couple: In *Lolita* the couple are Humbert and Lo; in *The Dangerous Husband,* narrator and frog.

Reading Group Questions and Topics for Discussion

1. During the dinner party where they first fall in love, the heroine tells her future husband, "Here's something I know: I am not going to kill. I mean unless it was in some extreme self-defense situation, to save my own life, and that's just normal. Otherwise, even if I felt abused or victimized, believe me, I'm not murdering anybody." How could this woman evolve into a potential murderer? Was she driven mad, or just pushed too far?

2. To the casual observer, Dennis is an ideal husband—adoring, attractive, affluent—and with him the narrator has an enviable life. Why then do you think she ends up falling in love with strangers instead of the husband who trips over himself to please her? Have you ever had a similar experience?

3. The female mugger, the woman in the restaurant rest room—female strangers automatically recognize the heroine's peril and her homicidal tendencies. Did you experience a flash of recognition here as well? Why is it that many women share that murderous impulse?

4. In many ways the narrator feels trapped, both figuratively and literally. (Even some of the doors to her house are nailed shut.) And yet during most of the story she's still physically able to leave. Why do you think she doesn't? When she does run away from home, why does she come back?

5. Did you find Dennis a completely sympathetic character, or an increasingly sinister one? Did your feelings

change when the heroine learned the fate of Dennis's three previous wives?

6. There's a lot of sex in this book, but as the story progresses, the couple's lovemaking sessions begin to end abruptly. Did you share the narrator's befuddlement? Why do you think Dennis leaves her in such a peculiar way?

7. Pets in this novel often end up the innocent victims of their owners. In what ways do they also represent their owners? How do their individual fates parallel their owners'?

8. As the story unfolds, this couple becomes increasingly isolated—their friends don't call them, the woman who introduced them claims not to have been involved. Is their loneliness their own doing, are they in fact unlikable people, or is it simply a condition of modern marriage?

9. The novel is presented in the form of a testimonial—the narrator is telling her story to an unseen audience, making an attempt to set the record straight. As she says early on, "Now, these two years later, I don't know much but I'll tell you all I know. You convict me if you will." To whom do you think she's speaking? Do you believe her version of the story?

10. There's a fairy-tale element to the story —Dennis is the handsome prince, he and his bride are poised to live happily ever after, there's even a wise frog offering advice. How much of the story as a whole did you think was pure fantasy? Was there a particular point where you felt the story departed from reality?

This Reading Group Guide to Jane Shapiro's *The Dangerous Husband* is also available at www.twbookmark.com

NEW FICTION IN PAPERBACK
Featuring Reading Group Guides

This Body
by Laurel Doud

"Lots of fun. . . . Every woman has had the fantasy of waking up in a younger, skinnier body. But what if you had to die first? And what if the body you came to one year after your death belonged to a freshly OD'd junkie?"
—Cindy Bagwell, *Dallas Morning News*

White Oleander
by Janet Fitch

"A truly gifted writer. . . . Astrid's journey is much, much more than the gripping, page-turning adventure of a young hero tripping through life. It is life."
—Warwick Downing, *Denver Post*

Hangover Soup
by Louise Redd

"A funny, sassy, sexy, moving book about love, sex, friendship, sports, education, alcoholism, marriage, and commitment; in short, something for everyone."
—Theodora Schmid, *Tampa Tribune-Times*

Fortune's Rocks
by Anita Shreve

"A deliciously intelligent page-turner. . . . A succulent novel of forbidden Victorian passion. . . . It has a morally complex heroine, a breakneck narrative, and an emotional story filled with unpredictable twists and turns."
—Jocelyn McClurg, *Hartford Courant*

Evening News
by Marly Swick

"An affecting novel . . . utterly palpable and real. . . . It possesses both the psychological suspense of Sue Miller's best-selling drama *The Good Mother* and the emotional acuity of Alice Munro's short stories."
—Michiko Kakutani, *New York Times*

Available wherever books are sold